# KEEPING HER SAFE

ALIE GARNETT

*To my my sister M who talked me into changing the ending, making it even better than before.*

# CHAPTER ONE

THE OCEAN WAS calm as the sun sank into the orange and red glow over the horizon. It was as if the man standing just out of reach of the waves was bending it to his will, forcing the waves to stop crashing into the shore.

He stood in the sand still in work shoes, coat slung over his back. He must've been holding it by the collar, probably with just one finger, but his back was in shadows. She couldn't be sure. Black dress slacks fluttered in the light breeze. He was like a god commanding the waves to cease for him.

Zephyr Hart sat watching the man who stared at the ocean beyond him. She had noticed him when he had shown up an hour ago, and he had been standing at the edge of the waves, watching the sunset the entire time. His head hadn't even glanced up or down the beach.

Did he know she was watching him? Did he know she was sitting on the deck? She hadn't moved since he'd arrived either, but she knew he knew she was there, and he had to have known she was watching him. Zachary Wainwright was a cop and a good one at that. He knew everything that went on around him.

What was he doing here? Was he making her wait for him to come to the house on purpose? Was he expecting her to come out to the beach? She didn't know, so she just stayed where she was.

If she had known he was coming, she would've worn something nicer than the gray sweatpants and a neon green oversized T-shirt she had on. But that was her usual attire, and he had come unannounced. He couldn't expect her to be all dressed up when he showed up unannounced.

As his toe kicked at the sand at his feet, Zephyr wondered if he was going to come see her. Maybe he just wanted to see the ocean. He loved the ocean, and he had practically grown up in the house behind her. He had spent more time there than she ever had during his childhood.

A red curl blew into her face, and she pushed it behind her ear with a sigh. What was he doing here? Zephyr hadn't seen him in almost two years. Not since his father's funeral. Not a great memory. She had lost the only person in the world who loved her that day. Brian Wainwright had been the closest thing to a father she'd ever had. Unfortunately, his only son had hated her since the first time they had met over a decade ago.

Zephyr had actually never thought she would see him again; he had said as much the day of the funeral. Brian had left Zachary everything he had but this beach house that he had given to Zephyr. At the time, Zephyr had been living in the beach house for two years, but when she heard what the will said, she told Zachary he could have the house. She could move out and find somewhere else to live. It was at that point he yelled at her to keep the house and that he would never darken its door again.

Then why was he standing in the sand in front of it right now? Was he here to start a fight again? Maybe she should start looking for a place to live instead of watching him watch the sunset.

The sun had finally sunk into the sea when Zachary turned away from the waves, and Zephyr watched him walk towards her in the twilight. His white shirt was unbuttoned, and the ends fluttered in the ocean breeze. Under his open shirt, he wore a white tank top that hugged his muscles.

As he drew closer, she noticed he hadn't changed in the last two years; he was still as good-looking as he'd always been. His tight, black curly hair was cut close to his head. It was longer than it had been when he was in the military, but still short by any standard. His skin was the color of light milk chocolate, and the white shirt made it seem more striking.

Zephyr watched him step up on the deck, throw his coat over the railing, and take the chair across from her. His brown eyes penetrated hers as he leaned back in the chair and looked at her.

"Zephyr."

"Zachary." She used the same irritated voice he had.

"I talked to Ken Jackson today." Not much segue there.

Ken Jackson was Zephyr's editor. He worked for the publishing company that published her books, and she had also talked to him yesterday. He had talked to her about there being a guy who was sending letters about something, but it hadn't mattered to her. All she cared about was finishing her latest book.

"Why did he call you?" she asked calmly.

"I talked to him in person, Zephyr. He called me to his office for a chat." Zachary's brown eyes were still on her.

"I don't think you two have anything to talk about," Zephyr told him. It was true because she couldn't see how they'd have anything in common.

"Apparently, I'm your next of kin," he said unemotionally.

Exhaling slowly, she replied, "I guess you are. I can take you off. I'll call him tomorrow."

His name had been the only one she could think of to put on the forms once Brian was gone. Even today, he was the person she most trusted in the world. No matter how little she saw him.

"Zephyr, this is serious." He sat up as he spoke, "The guy who's stalking you wants you dead."

She shook her head. "Nobody wants me dead."

"Zephyr, I've read the letters. He knows where you are and that you live here. And he knows you live alone." Zachary was taking this way too seriously.

Trying to keep calm, she rubbed her hands over her face, then lowered them to the table. "If it happens, it happens."

"Really, Zephyr, you're all okay with being dead? What about your fans?"

She lowered her hands to her lap. "They'll be fine. There are a ton of books they can read."

"But they want to read *yours*. You have one coming out in a month, and you have pre-sold over fifty thousand already. Which number is this?" He leaned back in his chair again.

"It's the eighth in the series."

It seemed odd, talking about her books with him. She never talked to anyone about her books. Nobody even knew she was an author. Not that she had many friends, but the few she did have had no clue. And her family comprised of just Zachary now. Not that he considered her family.

"You want there to be a ninth, right?" His eye's dark eyes were staring at her again. *What were they seeing?* she wondered.

"I have already written the next three, and I'm almost done with the next one," she told him calmly.

"How long is this series?" He looked more interested than she had ever thought he would be.

She smiled. "I'm on the last one, so thirteen."

He put his hand over his eyes. "You do realize, Zephyr Hart, that you are twenty-two-years-old. You've written thirteen books before most kids your age have finished college."

"I'm twenty-three, actually, and I had four done before I graduated from high school, so not as great of an accomplishment as you think." She didn't like praise.

He sat up quickly, and she saw a flash of anger in his eyes. "Don't you ever say what you have accomplished is nothing. I heard they were thinking about making a movie about the first one," Zachary said.

"That's just a rumor." She had heard nothing about making a movie.

"Every one of the books you've released has been on the bestsellers list, Zephyr. The rest will be, too. You are an amazing writer, so don't belittle what you've done."

"Have you read them?" She leaned towards him, betting money he hadn't.

"I started the first one," he admitted after a moment. "I have the next couple that were at Dad's when I cleaned out the place. I never got through it."

She smiled at him. "Those are worth money. First-edition signed copies. They're the only ones I've ever signed."

Her pen name was Z Connor. Connor was her middle name, so it had been an easy name to come up with when she showed up with her three first manuscripts at eighteen. Ken Jackson had told her it was perfect, that the kids wouldn't know if the writer was male or female. Her books hadn't been pigeon-holed as books for girls, even if her main characters were girls.

"I guess I have something to retire on then," he said with a laugh.

His whole body seemed to relax when he laughed. There hadn't been a lot of laughs between the two of them over the years, mostly just tension and anger. Maybe after this visit, they could be friends … or at least not enemies.

"Why are you here, Zachary?" she asked pointedly. So far, he had wasted a lot of her time, most of it watching him watch the ocean.

"I'm here to keep you safe from this guy." The laughter vanished from his eyes.

"I don't need you here."

"You won't be here, anyway. He knows you live here, remember?"

"Where am I going?" she demanded. She did not want to leave. This is where she lived.

"Tomorrow, we're going someplace else," he answered cryptically.

"I don't want to leave, Zachary," she whispered. The house was her sanctuary, and she had left it rarely in the last five years.

"You have to leave, Zephyr. You can work anywhere, but you're in danger here."

"You have to work. You're a big-time cop," she argued. She was *not* leaving.

"I've taken personal time. My little sister is in danger." He smiled at her.

"I am not your sister; you made sure of that," she hissed. Getting up, she walked into the house, leaving him sitting at the table. The same old tension reared its head in an instant. Once again, she couldn't be in the same room with him, and that included the entire outdoors.

# CHAPTER TWO

ZACHARY WATCHED HER LONG, curly red hair sway in concert with her backside as she walked into the house. Leaning back in the chair he closed his eyes and tried to get the image out of his mind. It was impossible when he was near her—she consumed him.

The harsh words were true, but he couldn't go back in time and fix his mistakes. It was him that had made her life so horrible that she'd turned inward to the books she wrote. With one sentence at nineteen, he had altered the course of her life, changing her forever.

When he looked back on that day, he used to see some punk kid who wanted to take his place in his father's heart and life. But with age, he could now see that she was just a scared kid who had nothing but his dad on her side. Everything she had was gone.

Brian had spent months working on the paperwork and legal aspects of adopting the twelve-year-old red-headed girl. She'd lost her mother in a bar fight less than a year before and had nobody in her life. Everything that had been done had been for nothing when Zachary took the stand and told the judge that he didn't want a sister. It was a week before he was deployed to Afghanistan for the first time, and he'd seen his father moving on to another kid. Where did that leave Zachary, his first kid?

By the time Zachary had returned two years later, Zephyr was gone, thrown into a foster system that had broken her. He remembered her as outgoing and easy to make laugh, but the girl had turned into a quiet cautious teenager.

He had been right here at the beach house when Brian had brought her down for the weekend. It seems his dad could talk her foster parents into letting him take the girl a few weekends a year. Brian, of course, would bring her to the ocean. His dad had loved the ocean and loved sharing it with his kids, which was why he owned a beach house when he was only a cop.

When Zachary had first seen her that day, she was sitting at the same table she had been sitting at today. That day she was writing in a notebook. He noticed that when she wrote, she sometimes didn't even look at the paper. She'd just stare off in space, and the pen would just go in straight, even lines across the page.

That day she had to have been close to fifteen. Her body had filled out since he had last seen her. No longer was she stick-skinny and short. That day he noticed that her breasts had come in, and they were bigger than any fifteen-year-old needed. All weekend she mostly wore a sweatshirt and sometimes a T-shirt, but only when the temperatures soared. He knew she was hiding her body, which was probably something she had learned by living with men who were not afraid to stare.

It wasn't just her bombshell body that had taken him aback that weekend, but that she was guarded at all times. When he and Brian talked, she rarely joined in. When Brian joked around with her, she didn't laugh anymore. Her personality had changed, and Zachary knew it was his fault. He knew how bad the foster system was on kids, and it was worse for girls.

Ken, her editor, had told him that she rarely left the house and never went on tour for her books—she didn't even want people to know she wrote them. Ken was concerned for her about more than just the threats to her life. The editor thought she was hiding in the beach house. Hiding from the world.

When Ken had told him that he was her next of kin and executor of her estate, he wanted to cry. All he could see was the woman she could have been if it hadn't been for his selfishness. This wasn't the way she was supposed to be.

Rubbing his hands over his short, curly hair, he thought about her as his sister. What would that picture look like when Brian showed it around? A short and pale red-headed daughter and an African American son. Nobody would believe they were related.

Getting up, he walked into the house and saw she was washing dishes in the sink. Her sweatpants didn't hide the round curve of her hips. He scolded himself to not look at her that way, but he couldn't help it.

He first saw her as desirable back when he saw her for the first time in years when his father was dying. He had gotten a text from his father's phone, telling him he'd father had been shot, and he had gotten there as fast as he could. Now he knew Zephyr had written the text. By the time he had shown up, he was too late. Brian was no longer there, but his body still lay in the bed. After hugging the man who had raised him, he looked up and saw her standing in front of the window. Her back was to them, giving them privacy.

All he saw as he held his father for the last time was an angel standing in streams of sunlight. It bounced off her red curls, making them look like they were on fire. Her shoulders were bare, and he could see pale skin peeking out from the wild strands of fire.

Before he knew what he was doing, he had walked over to her and pulled her into his arms. When he felt her arms go around him, he realized he had stopped breathing. At that moment, he felt alive.

Running a hand up her back, he pulled her closer to him, and he sighed when her head rested against his chest. He felt her sigh in return as he rested his cheek on her hair. Suddenly, he loved how small she was, how well she fit in his arms.

To this day, he didn't know how long they stayed that way—moments, hours. It felt like mere seconds, and then it was over. A nurse rushed in and started talking to them. Zephyr pulled out of his arms as the nurse spoke, but Zachary didn't want her to leave. Relenting, he let her go and hadn't touched her since, but his body craved her touch.

"Zephyr, I'm sorry. I was a young, dumb kid then. I know what I said was wrong. I can't fix it for you," Zachary pleaded with her, not for the first time.

"I can't forgive you, Zachary. That was my only chance out of the system. I never even got close again." She didn't turn away from her washing, but her hands had stopped moving in the water. She was standing perfectly still.

"I am sorry, Zephyr," he said again, knowing it wasn't enough.

"Just drop it, Zachary. Just forget it," she replied. "Can we just pretend that we don't have a history? It isn't a good one anyway."

"If that's what you want. Let's start again." He got up and walked halfway to her, then put out his hand and said, "Zachary Wainwright."

Turning, she saw him standing there, looking at her expectantly. Grabbing a towel, she dried her hands and walked over. The hand she placed in his was slightly damp and warm from the water, and the touch warmed him to his toes. Desire instantly settled in his groin, as she answered, "Zephyr Hart."

He still held her hand and did want to let go, but he asked, "What do you do for a living?"

"I am a writer." Her blue eyes were twinkling at him. "How about you?"

Smiling down at her, he said, "I am a cop, but right now, I am on assignment to keep Zephyr Hart alive."

Her eyes dropped from his, and she pulled her hand away. She walked away from him and back to the sink but didn't put her hands in the water. "I am not in danger, Zachary. I think I would know if someone was going to kill me."

"You're the writer, Zephyr. I'm the cop. You write your little stories, and I will make sure you are safe. One week—we'll come back in one week. Can you give me that?"

Turning back to him, she leaned against the sink. "One week only, nothing more."

"Nothing more, Zeph."

"It's Zephyr. Always has been."

"Okay, *Zephyr*." He emphasized her name. "One week."

"If we can't stay here, where will we go?" She smiled at him, crossing her arms over her ample chest.

"Minnesota," he said with a smile.

At the word, her face lost the beautiful smile, and her eyes glared at him. All she said was, "No."

"I didn't say where, Zephyr. It's a big state."

"It's winter there."

"Nobody will look for you in the snow," he teased.

"I don't do winter." Her voice was firm.

"I think you will like it." His was upbeat.

"Don't do this, Zachary. Anywhere else. I'll even pay. Can't we go anywhere else?"

"Minnesota."

"California? To see the other ocean?"

"Minnesota," he said again, shaking his head.

"Washington? See the rain?" She offered.

"Minnesota."

"Nebraska? I have no idea what we would see there … farms?" Her ideas were running dry.

"Minnesota?" he said again. "They have plenty of farms to see."

"Why?" she demanded.

"Because you need to go there once," he said simply.

"I've done just fine without ever going there."

"Nobody will ever think to look for you there," he insisted.

She started biting her bottom lip. "I don't want to go there."

"Let's just go. Maybe you can see them. You don't have to introduce yourself. I think you need to just see it … see them." He looked into her large blue eyes, trying not to watch her biting her lip—trying not to think about biting that lip himself.

"I don't want to know them," she whispered.

"Just look and see if there's anything there for you."

Her lip quivered. "They don't know about me."

"Then they won't be looking for you. You can introduce yourself or walk away, whichever you want. But I think you need to do this, Zephyr." He nodded.

"Please, Zachary, don't make me do this."

He watched a single tear roll down her cheek. At that moment, he wanted to take it all back, gather her in his arms, and never make her do anything she didn't want to do. Before he could say a word, she pushed herself away from the counter and walked to the bedroom. She paused at the door, but then walked into it and shut the door behind her.

It would take everything inside him to get her on that plane going north. Though he didn't know the entirety of her past, his dad had told him a little. It was years after Brian had tried to adopt Zephyr, but she wasn't yet eighteen. Brian had asked him to stop by; it had come out of the blue since Zachary had just started on the force that year.

Sitting in the back yard, across from this father in his home in Tampa, it had surprised Zachary when the older man had said, "Zephyr's father died today."

Zachary had been stunned. Where was this man five years ago? "I didn't know she had one."

Brian put his beer down and replied, "He was married to her mother when Zephyr was born but signed away his rights as soon as he could."

"What about when her mom died?" Zachary asked.

"That was after she was dead. I told him she would end up in foster care, but he didn't care. He was tired of raising his wife's kids."

"Bastard," Zachary hissed, hurting for the red head.

"Yeah, but now he's dead. Her next of kin is now a few sisters, all adults."

"Do you think they will want her?" He wanted to know.

"I don't know. I don't know if I can take the chance with Zephyr. She's special, Zach." He looked at the dead grass in the yard.

"Yeah, I guess," Zachary mumbled. At the time, he had seen nothing too special about her.

"She's six months from turning eighteen. She's been writing for years—you know that. Always writing something. She's finished three books already, and they're good. I told her not to publish them until she was eighteen and out of the system. I want her work to be hers," Brian explained.

He went on, "I don't want to tell these women that they have a sister, and they just use her for her talent, stealing everything she ever did. She's not of age yet, so they could."

"So, you think these women will just take advantage of her?" Zachary asked, brows scrunching together in contemplation.

"I don't know. Does it make me a bad person for wanting to guard her future, or am I being a bad person for sending her to people she doesn't know? Which makes me the worse person?"

"Does she know she has sisters?" Zachary asked.

"Yes, her mom used to talk about them a lot."

"Has she ever tried to contact them?"

"No, they don't know about her."

"Then I think you leave things as they are. If she wants to contact her sisters, she can. That way, she'll be able to control her own future," Zachary replied confidently.

Both men fell silent as they drank their beer. Each was lost in thought. Cars drove by, and neighbor kids yelled in the distance as they sat silently. Zachary couldn't help but wonder about a man who would cast a child into the system. Didn't he know how bad it was for a kid alone in the world?

Brian set his beer on the patio table. It was empty. Turning to his son, he said, "If something happens to me, I need you to take care of Zephyr. She needs someone, and I want you to be that someone, Zachary."

"Okay, Dad, I'll take care of her. But you have to promise that it won't happen for many years," he joked. His father was putting a lot of responsibility on his only son.

Brian didn't laugh as he looked at the empty can on the table. "Zachary, do you remember when you were eighteen, and I took you up north to Jacksonville and found your mom's grave?"

Zachary looked at the man who had done everything for him. "Yes."

"I want to take Zephyr to her mom's hometown one day, maybe

meet her sisters. I think she really does need to meet them at least once. If I don't live long enough, I want you to take her. Birch Cove, Minnesota—remember that. Her family's names are the same as hers: Hart."

"Why so much talk about dying tonight, Dad?" Zachary asked.

"I don't know, just feeling down today. Will you take her?" he asked again.

"Yes. I will take her, I promise," Zachary said with a nod.

Brian grabbed his hand and held it for a while, then said, "She's your sister, even if I didn't get to adopt her. She's been my daughter for years now."

"I know, Dad, and I'm sorry."

Brian hadn't excepted his apology that day or any other day. The older man had died, never forgiving his son for that day. Now, Zachary could only apologize to Zephyr in hopes she would one day forgive him.

As he had sat in Ken Jackson's office, listening to the man tell him Zephyr was not taking their threats seriously, he knew that he had to keep her safe. He had promised his father to take care of the woman and for two years hadn't even thought of her down in the beach house. Now she needed him, and he would do everything in his power to keep her safe. Even if she didn't want him to.

After reading the threatening letters, he had known she was not safe in Florida at all. When he tried to think of a place to take her, the only place that came to mind was Minnesota. Nobody would look for her way up north. The only ties she had to the state was that her mother had been born there, but few people knew that. He knew it was the perfect time to finally bring her to her hometown.

He instantly agreed to keep her safe because it was the job his father had given him. When he had asked Ken who he thought the stalker could be, the list was small. Zephyr knew almost nobody. No exes, no former friends with an ax to grind. In fact, he had told Zachary that he was at the top of the list. Zachary had complete control of her money if she died—which no one had thought to mention to him before then.

When he had gotten back to his office, he had looked up all three of the sisters. None had anything in their past that showed that they would be dangerous. In fact, all three lived in the same small town they had been raised in. One of them had been in the Army, but since then, they'd barely left the state. None of them had been out of Minnesota in over a year. Following the trail, he looked into their husbands, and all were perfectly normal people.

Then he focused on the woman in question: Zephyr Connor Hart. She was twenty-three and lived alone in a house on the beach. She had never graduated from high school, earning a GED instead, and had never had a job except writing … ever. She had never flipped burgers, waited tables, or rung up clothing sales. Zephyr was a writer. The woman had no Facebook page, Twitter account, or presence on the internet at all.

Turning to Zephyr's pen name, Zachary hit a gold mine. Z Connor had a web page, a Facebook page, many fan forums, and the books were for sale everywhere. He could see how popular her books were— millions loved them. There was a page with a countdown to the release of the next book, but he found nothing out of the ordinary; nothing that seemed threatening.

Ken had been right. Zachary was on the top of the list. He was one of the few people who knew her and who she was. He could get close to her, and she didn't fear him. And they didn't get along.

With a sigh, he shook his head. Right now, he needed to concentrate on the present, not the past. He ran out to his car and grabbed the duffle bag with his clothes in it. He would stay on her couch tonight, and tomorrow, they were out of here. Maybe he should have insisted they leave tonight, but he was here to keep her safe for one more day.

# CHAPTER THREE

ZEPHYR WAS TRYING to type on the laptop in front of her, but the words were gone. They were stuck in her head, unable to get through the memories racing through her mind. Slamming the machine shut, she pushed it away from her. No use to even try working. It was only editing anyway.

Minnesota was all she could think of. The cold, arctic birthplace of her family. Zephyr had never been there. In fact, she had never been out of Florida. She'd never been to Georgia, Alabama, or Mississippi, nor had she ever been on a plane. Maybe taking a boat was a way out, but she could not swim and was terrified of the water.

It made perfect sense that she owned a beach house right on the ocean. Every day she went and poked her toes in the wet sand and let the waves run over her feet, but it had been years since the saltwater had touched her knees.

Her mom had said that in Minnesota, it got cold enough there that it wouldn't snow. *How cold was that?* Was it that cold there now? It was October, so it was probably cold enough to snow, but not too cold that it wouldn't snow? Zephyr had never seen snow in real life.

Her mom had also said that Minnesota smelled different from

here. Would she be able to smell the difference? What does that even mean?

Minnesota was where her mom had spent her first thirty-two years of life. She had been raised there, gotten married there, given birth to three girls there, and had left there. Left all of it behind. She had only taken Zephyr with her, small and maybe unwanted in her stomach as she fled the state. Never did Catherine Hart return to Minnesota, and never had she taken Zephyr there.

All Zephyr knew about Minnesota was what her mom had told her about it. The big house she had been raised in with her loving mom and dad, both long dead; the green farm that she lived in with her husband and raised her daughters in. Apparently, her mother had hated the quietness of the farm.

Minnesota was the home of her three sisters, who never knew she existed. But Zephyr knew they existed—her mom talked about them all the time. Everything Zephyr did was compared to the ghosts of her unknown siblings. Zephyr had red hair like Della and Zoey. Zephyr had Evie's nose. Zephyr walked later than Della, but earlier than the other two. Zephyr talked later than Zoey but before the other two. Zephyr would be short, like the girls. Zephyr wasn't outgoing like Zoey. Zephyr wasn't smart like Della. Zephyr wasn't pretty like Evie. Zephyr was never better than the girls. Kate had always called them 'the girls.' The girls.

Kate had left behind the girls to raise Zephyr, whose father hadn't wanted to raise another of Kate's mistakes. Zephyr knew she was that mistake her entire life. She had known her mother would have gone back to her girls if it hadn't been for Zephyr. She had known her mom wasn't happy raising her; she wanted to raise the other three. Every word she had said to her baby girl had been about how Zephyr wasn't as good as her girls, and never would be.

Minnesota. Zephyr had spent twelve years hearing about it, wondering about it, and dreaming about it. Now she was going to it. Would she see snow? Would she see the farm? Would she see the girls?

Pulling the blanket over her, she snuggled into her bed. Zachary had turned the TV on in the living room. Apparently, he was staying on the couch. The house had only one bedroom. If she were a braver soul, she would've invited him into her bedroom. For comfort? For sex? Either one would be fine as long as it was Zachary.

It's not like she would ever act on her feelings for him. She was neither his type nor in his league. She had been fifteen years old when he came home from Afghanistan. He was all man, muscle, and swim shorts, and he had been the ideal man in her mind. Nobody ever measured up to him.

The few men she had dated were either too short, didn't have brown eyes, or wore their hair too long. It had gotten worse after Brian had died. Suddenly, the men she had dated needed to be muscular, and if they were darker-skinned, they got a plus. But none had ever made it past the first date because none of them had been Zachary.

Zephyr was well aware she was being stupid. Zachary couldn't stand her, and she just yearned for him. But then again, only Zachary could make her insides turn to mush with only a glance in her direction. When they had shaken hands this evening, she felt tingles running through her body, from her toes to her nose, and especially in her lady bits.

How was she going to spend a week with him—a week? She was going to throw herself at him, and he was going to look down his perfect nose at her pathetic moves. He would probably leave her in the cold tundra of Minnesota.

Groaning, she turned the light off beside her and flopped onto her stomach. This would be the hardest week she'd ever get through. *Even harder than Zachary's chiseled abs.*

# CHAPTER FOUR

SOFT SCRAPING at the door woke Zachary from his light sleep. In an instant, he rolled onto the floor, gun in hand, and crawled to the bedroom door. The scraping came again as he pushed the door open to the dark bedroom. Silently, he closed the door behind him. With speed, he crawled over to the bed. "Zephyr," he whispered as he reached for her in the bed.

His heart stopped when he heard the front door open with a squeak, and Zachary realized the bed was empty and cold. Where was she? Glancing at the bathroom door, he saw it was open, and was empty. Scanning the room, he saw a faint light coming from the closet. Jumping to his feet, he ran to the door and pulled it open, hoping it did not squeak. Lucking out, the doors silently opened to reveal Zephyr sitting against the wall, computer open on her lap, and giant headphones on her head. Faint music hummed from the headphones.

At the sight of him, her blue eyes grew wide behind round glasses in the light from the computer screen. Her mouth opened in an 'O,' but no words were spoken. In one move, he was in the closet with her, pulling the door shut behind him.

Turning with his gun in hand, he slowly closed the laptop, plunging the closet into darkness. He was practically sitting on top of her, holding the gun in his hands, pointing it at the door inches from his face. Behind him, he could feel Zephyr squirm, so he shifted slightly so that he wasn't pushing her into the wall behind them.

The music had stopped when he had shut the computer, and he saw her pulling off the headphones from the corner of his eye. His eyes were focused on the unopened door. She was squirming again, and he realized he was pushing her into the wall. Instantly, she stopped moving when they heard the bedroom door creak open.

Suddenly, Zachary was torn. Should he stay in the closet and protect Zephyr or rush the guy and maybe let her get hurt? Or worse. The answer was as obvious as the nose on his face: he had to keep Zephyr safe, even if it meant letting this guy walk today.

As Zachary listened to the man walking through the room behind the door, he could feel the heat from her body. Somehow, he had trapped her entire upper body between him and the wall. Her face was just behind his shoulder, and he could feel her breath on the bare skin of his back.

Silently, he chastised himself for being stupid enough to go to bed in just underwear. But the house had been so hot he didn't think he would be able to sleep in anything else. Had he not thought the threat was real or just not immediate?

As the moments ticked by, Zephyr placed her hand on his bare thigh, and the touch nearly made him jump. How was he going to be ready when the door opened if all he could concentrate on was her hand on his thigh and her breasts against his back? He silently cursed as he felt blood rush to his groin. He would blame it on the situation out of the closet, not in it.

The footsteps made their way closer to them. Silently, he leaned back into Zephyr, hearing her squeak as he did. Before he could think about his plan, he raised his foot and kicked at the closed door with all the strength he had. The door flew off the hinge, sending the intruder sprawling back onto the bed.

Zachary had them out of the closet and across the room before the man had fully landed on the bed. Whoever it was had left the door open, and Zephyr yanked it closed behind her has he pulled her along.

"Out," he whispered at her. Why had he whispered? The guy knew they were there.

Grabbing his pants, he turned to make sure she was following, but she wasn't. There she was, cradling her computer and reaching toward a shelf just out of her reach for something. Running over to her, he demanded, "What?"

"Vase."

He spotted the old, ugly, green vase and grabbed it. "Now *out*."

Following behind, he almost ran into her as she grabbed shoes from the floor by the door. Once they were outside, he glanced at her car to see the tires were flat. He led her to his car, which was parked on the street. He reached into his pants' pocket and pulled out the keys, unlocked it, and hurried in.

He had it started in gear and moving before Zephyr got her door closed. After pulling out onto the street, he had the car doing fifty as he ran three red lights. It was just after four in the morning, and the streets were still completely empty.

Checking the rearview mirror, he saw nobody was following, but he wasn't taking his chances at this time. He was driving fast and on pure adrenalin.

Once they were two blocks from the house, he pulled out his phone and contacted his partner from work. Travis had known Zachary had taken the job of protecting Zephyr, though Travis didn't really know who she was, just that the two of them had known each other through Brian. He informed his partner about the break-in, and Travis promised to get down there and look into the situation himself and report back to Zachary. With that, he hung up.

They had made it halfway from her beach house to his house in Tampa before he looked at his passenger. The small woman was still hugging the computer and vase to her chest. It surprised him she was not crying or reacting at all.

"Are you okay, Zeph?"

"Yes." Her voice was a little shaky.

"Why the vase?"

She didn't answer his question, but instead asked, "What happened to you?"

He looked at her, eyebrow raised. "What? Someone tried to kill you, Zephyr."

"No, you have a pretty extensive bandage there." Her eyes were looking at it as she spoke.

To his surprise, he hadn't even noticed the wound during the ordeal in the closet, but now it was making itself known. Yesterday was the first day he hadn't had pain from it. Today, it was going to bother him a little.

"I was shot last week on the job," he replied coolly.

"Why didn't you tell me?" she whispered.

"Because I didn't die, and we weren't exactly talking before yesterday."

"Would they have called me if you died, or would I have had to hear about it on the news?" her voice was small.

He paused before answering, "I don't know, probably the news."

"When you go back, I want you to tell them to call me. I want to know if something happens to you." He could hear the tears in her voice now.

"I will, Zeph," he said softly. Reaching out, he ran a hand over her riot of red curls.

"Zephyr." She looked away from him and out the window into the darkness.

He corrected himself. "Zephyr."

"Now what?" She was still looking out the window.

"Now, we head north."

She looked at him, her face a mask of worry. "Zachary, we have nothing. I don't even have my license or credit cards."

Before he could answer, they had pulled into his garage. After closing the door behind them, he cut the engine and said, "Stay here. I'll be just a minute. Then we leave again."

He needed clothes, and he had left his travel bag on the floor in the beach house. Running through the house, he grabbed a spare duffle bag from the closet and started filling it with enough clothes for seven days in the cold. Halfway through, he realized he was still in his underwear and pulled on a pair of jeans, not bothering to button or zip them. There would be time later for that.

With the bag full, he went into the closet and opened his gun safe, needing a case for the gun he carried, as well as a second gun and case. Each gun needed a case for the flight, and he could bring them as long as they were in a checked bag in a case.

"Can I put something in there?" Zephyr asked, and he nearly jumped out of his skin. Somehow, she had silently walked into the house and into his bedroom without him hearing her.

Once again, she was in gray sweatpants, but tighter than the ones from yesterday. The yellow T-shirt said 'Florida' across her breasts. The outfit and the wild, curly hair made her look young and vulnerable. Yesterday, it had been bound with a tie, but today it was free, and it seemed to be taking every advantage to run wild.

"What?" he asked.

"This." She held out the green vase.

"Sure," he said, reaching for it. "Is it full of money, Zephyr? Don't you trust the banks?"

"No, not money. It's the USB drives with all my books on them," she replied.

He had the vase in his hand when she had said the words. His hand started shaking at the weight of what he was holding. Millions of dollars were on these USB drives. Maybe billions.

"Do you think it'll be safe here?" he asked, moving a few guns to make room for it.

"No, but it's all I have right now."

He looked at the vase in the safe and took it out again. He walked out of the closet with the vase and a handgun in his hand. On the bed, he opened the gun case and took the gun out of it. Slowly he dumped the vase contents into the empty case. He saw there were around twenty USB drives in total. "Are these the only copies?"

"No, my publisher has another set of copies, but these are mine." Her eyes were on him, but she didn't ask what he was doing.

"Do you want to bring them with us or leave them here?" he asked, holding the now-closed gun case between them.

"Here."

"The safe?"

"No, he would look there." She said the words that were running through his head.

"Where?"

She answered by taking the case and leaving the room, and he followed her into the bedroom next door. It had once been his bedroom, but now it contained an office. He realized this was also the room she would have slept in when visiting Brian. In the closet, she pulled out a few boxes that sat on the floor of his old things, boxes that had been there for years. When the boxes were out, she crawled in and came back without the case.

Smiling at her, he said, "I'll put the boxes back. Did you take out my nudy magazines?" He knew the hollow spot under the carpet that was big enough for a few magazines.

"Years ago. When I was in high school, I stored all my books in there," she said as she watched him pile the boxes back in. Her work was back in the same spot it had started in.

"We have to go. We've stayed here too long."

He needed them to get going before he spent too much time staring at her in his childhood bedroom, realizing she had slept in his bed dozens of times. Though the bed was gone, the picture of her in it was crystal clear. It didn't help that she was standing in the middle of the room and biting her lip like a nervous teenager.

"Zephyr, we have to go," he repeated. This time he forced himself to leave her in the room. Throwing on a T-shirt, he stuffed the last of his things in his bag, then picked it up and turned around to leave.

She had followed him and was standing in the doorway. All he wanted to do was grab her into his arms and never let go; never let anything bad ever happen to her. What he did was physically turned her around and push her out of the door and down the hallway.

"Zachary, do you have a sweatshirt I can wear?" she asked as he pushed her along.

"Zephyr, I have nothing that will fit you." His hands were on her back, and he felt her stiffen at his words. He didn't have time to decode women tonight. He needed to get this city behind them as soon as possible.

Over the next hour, they made it out of the city and into the open countryside. Since he wasn't taking interstates, the trip would take longer than it usually did, but Zephyr said nothing during the drive, staying silent since they'd left his house. She was still clenching the computer to her chest.

As the second hour wore on, his phone rang. It was Travis, and he had no useful information at the beach house and nothing to identify the guy. The guy was long gone.

To Travis, he said, "I need you to book two seats out of Miami around 11:00 a.m. To Minneapolis. Yes, me and the Mrs." After he said it he hung up on his partner.

After a few minutes, Zephyr said, "I can't go on a plane."

"Can't or won't?"

"Can't. I have no ID. I left my wallet behind."

"I have identification for you," he said. She was never going to travel under her real name. What's the use leaving if the trail to find her was so easy?

"Okay, I also have no clothes. I can't go in public like this," she protested, vaguely gesturing to herself.

"Half the women on the plane will be in sweats. It's fine." He gave her an encouraging smile. "We'll buy you clothes when we get there."

"Can we stop and get a sweatshirt or something?"

"No, but we can get one at the airport. It'll only be a few hours."

"Do we need gas before then?" she leaned over to look at his dashboard.

"No, we have a full tank, which should be plenty." He noticed that every time he shot her idea down, she would nibble on her lip.

"Are the shops at the airport before or after all the lines?" she asked.

"After."

Again, she fell silent. Something was bothering her. Was it the break-in? Was it finally dawning on her how much danger she was in?

"Zephyr, what's the matter? Something's bothering you."

"Nothing," Zephyr mumbled.

"Come on, Zephyr, talk to me. We have around two more hours in this car together," he said and tapped her shoulder with his fist.

"It's nothing you would understand." She looked out the passenger window.

"Try me."

"I'm not wearing a bra. I should have put one on, but sometimes I don't," she whispered at the window.

"Women don't wear bras all the time, Zephyr," he reminded her gently.

"Not me. You don't understand, Zachary," she said again.

"Tell me then. Why does it matter?" He didn't understand what she was talking about. Her breasts were large and beautiful. He had spent hours last night trying not to think about them, trying not to wonder what they would feel like in his hands.

"People are always staring at them. Since the day they came in, it has been the first thing people notice about me: Zephyr with the red hair and big boobs. Strangers look and comment. I never go out without a bra on; they bounce when I walk. If I have another layer, maybe it wouldn't be as bad, but I really don't want to go to an airport with just this shirt on," she answered, never taking her eyes off the passenger window.

"I never knew." Zachary put his hand on her shoulder. He could hear the pain in her voice.

"That I had big boobs?" she asked, turning to look at him.

"I knew that, Zephyr. I have been well aware of that for years. I didn't know that they could be a curse and not a blessing. Most women don't have the problem of people staring all the time, but maybe it isn't the boobs that people are staring at," he said, not taking his hand off her shoulder.

"Thanks. So apparently, I'm so weird, people cannot help but stare at me." She turned back towards the window.

He saw his words hurt her, and he saw her eyes had filled with tears before she turned back to the window.

"Zephyr Hart, you are a beautiful woman. The first thing I notice about you is your glorious red hair. You have absolutely no control of it, and it flies everywhere. Even when you have it tied back, there are always strands that get away. Then I notice your pale skin. It reminds me of the cream I pour in my coffee in the morning. You never tan; you just turn red. You have three known freckles, not like some redheads. Three: one by your lip, one on your ear, and one on your left shoulder." He touched the freckle on her shoulder to emphasize the point.

"Then I'm usually consumed by these giant blue eyes of yours. I have yet to meet anyone with eyes that are so light blue, but there's a dark ring around them right at the outside edge. Then sometimes I get to see you smile and sometimes, just sometimes, that smile actually makes your eyes twinkle. That's when I know you're really happy."

He knew he had said too much. He was actually telling her what he saw every time he looked at her, except the parts where he wanted to bury his hands in her hair and see if it would curl around his fingers on its own. Nor did he mention how he wanted to touch her pale skin to see the difference in their skin tones. Would the combination really look like that split second after he poured creamer in his cup, where light and dark haven't combined yet, just swirled together?

They had been driving for almost an hour, and he was just realizing that he had not buttoned his pants before getting in the car. If she looked away from the window and looked at his crotch, she would see how much just looking at her got to him. His penis was well beyond half-mast, and he wondered how he would get it under control.

"But then you notice the breasts because they are a big part of me," she said playfully.

Though she didn't turn from the window, he knew she was making a joke. She had actually said a joke.

"Oh, honey, I know they're there. I'm not supposed to notice, but I have." He laughed.

# CHAPTER FIVE

WAS THE CAR GETTING HOT, or was it just her? Had Zachary looked at her breasts because they were there or because he wanted to? The shoulder he was touching got chilled when he pulled his hand away. She had no idea what to say, so she kept silent, and he also let the car be quiet.

The sun had risen, and the colors and sights of the countryside met her eyes. As the miles ticked by, she looked out the window at each passing house. Yards, garages, barns, sheds, each was unique, and each was the same. Some were interesting enough that a story of its occupants, past or present, ran through her mind. One old house caught her eye, and she wondered if the family that lived there noticed it needed paint or had they just bought it and hadn't had time to do the work yet? Each new house was a thirty-second story in her mind before she passed another, and the last one was forgotten.

"What are you thinking about over there?" Zachary's voice was loud after the long silence.

"Whether the people in these houses notice us as we drive by. Do they glance up and listen to the sound of our tires on the road? Do they look out the window to see if it is anyone they know, then be slightly disappointed when it is a stranger? Do they not even notice the sight or sound anymore, just another car passing by just like the last one, and another one will be here soon?" she wondered out loud.

"All I am thinking is that's a nice house, and that one is not. Nothing deep," he replied.

"I wonder what it would have been like to grow up in that house. Would I have had a bedroom upstairs? Would I have had a horse? A dog? Maybe just a cat. What would it be like to live in it now? Would I think I should paint it? Mow the lawn? How would I have gotten to the point of buying it, would I own it? How would my life be today if I had been raised there?" she said as more houses passed the windows.

"That's why you're a writer, Zephyr. I've never thought about any of that. Ever."

She looked over at him. "I'm a writer because I have never done anything else."

"What was the worst job you ever had, Zephyr?" he asked to keep her talking.

"Writing," she answered honestly. "You?"

"When I was sixteen, I worked at a burger shack on the beach. I made the French fries. Hottest, grossest job ever. War was better than that job," he replied with a laugh. "Best job?"

"Writing," she answered again, smiling this time. "You?"

"Being a cop. I love it. Being a beat cop wasn't as much fun as being a detective. I love helping people. Sometimes it gets to me when the bad guy gets off, but then I just have to get him again for something else."

His smile always made her heart beat faster. She didn't get to see it much. She could count on both hands the number of times in her life she had seen him smile, really smile.

"But it's dangerous," she added, eyeing the bandage she knew was under his shirt.

Letting her eyes slide down from the bandage, she noticed that his pants were not buttoned. His black underwear was peeking out of the opening. *Eyes back on the road*, she demanded herself.

As the road stretched out in front of them, her mind raced back to the closet in the beach house. When he had opened the door to the closet, she had been in there for almost an hour. When she had woken in the middle of the night, she had been unable to sleep. Not because he was in the house, but because she never went back to sleep after waking in the night. Over the years, she had learned she works best in the middle of the silent night. With headphones on to block the quiet of the house, she was able to let the stories flow like water.

Not wanting to disturb him, she had gone into the closet. Brian had once told her Zachary was a light sleeper, so she went to the only place she could think to get away from him. He probably thought she was crazy.

It had only taken her seconds to realize he had a gun and was nearly naked in front of her. Her breath was gone even before he slammed his body into hers.

His hard muscles had pushed her into the back of the closet with more strength than she could deal with. It took all her will not to make noise as her breasts were crushed between their bodies. She had tried to get a little relief, but he just kept shifting and grinding her into the wall. Now she wished she had concentrated on his nearly naked body instead of the pain, but at the time, only the pain registered.

It wasn't until they were in the car that she could think and notice him driving through town in his black boxers. His entire body was on display for her, almost every inch of it open to her gazing—if she had been bold enough to get more than a peak in.

"Are you saying the only job you have ever had was writing?" His voice pulled her back to now.

"Yes." Her voiced sounded hoarse, even to her.

"I want the long answer," Zachary said with a chuckle.

"Okay. Let's see. I don't remember a time when I wasn't writing. Once I knew how to make a sentence, I was putting them together to put the stories in my mind on paper. It was kind of a hobby I did when my mom was working. She was a waitress. She worked at a café during the day and at a bar on Friday and Saturday nights. Once I turned eight, she left me alone when she worked. I couldn't leave the apartment. That's when I started to write, turn on the radio, and put the stories on paper."

"She left you alone when you were eight? The law is twelve." He slowly let out a breath and said, "Go on."

"By the time she died, I was pretty much on my own all the time. She had started working at the bar every day. Sometimes, I wouldn't see her for days when she would start drinking. She didn't always remember she had a kid when she drank by that time. Anyway, she died, and I was still just writing when I was bored. I had written a lot of stuff, but nothing important. When I ended up in the first foster home, it was bad. There were six kids from the system there, and the mom worked all the time. She had an office job but was able to put in a lot of overtime. The dad liked to drink and watch TV, but when the lights went out, he liked to get handsy with the kids—any of them. I tried to stay in my room and away from him, but he would come in anyway. I shared it with two other girls. I may have been twelve, but I knew that look. I took off and ran as far as I could. I spent the night on the beach and by morning, a cop had picked me up." She stopped. "You don't care about that."

"Yes, Zephyr, I want to know."

"The cop took me to the station and called the social worker. I asked for your dad since he had been good to me when Mom died. He made it to me before the social worker did. By the time the social worker got there, he had a family lined up to take me in. They were nice. It lasted for a while, but then I went to another. But if I felt uncomfortable, Brian would get me moved. If the foster dad leered at me, I left. My boobs were an issue sometimes." Why did she have to keep bringing them into it?

"Men are pigs. You were talking about writing." He laughed.

"Oh, yeah, so when I was in all those foster homes, I would go to my room and write to escape. Let my mind take me to better places and better lands. When I was fifteen, I don't know why or how, but I started the Traveler series. First, it started with one book ... one journey. Then it turned into two, and so on. I would long-hand write at night and type it out in the computer lab at school during the day.

Soon I wasn't getting enough computer time, and the notebooks were piling up. Then in my junior year, I got two free hours in the computer lab a day. I was able to start whipping through the notebooks. Then in my senior year, I could get four hours; half a day. I know Brian had something to do with it. He wanted to get me my own computer, but we both knew it would be stolen in a week." She chuckled at her past predicament.

"When I was seventeen, I had three books complete and was working on another one and reviewing the fourth. I wanted to find a publisher and see if they would be interested or if I was wasting my time. Brian helped me find a few, and I submitted a sample. Within weeks, there were three companies that wanted me. Harry Potter was big then, so fantasy was hot. With your dad's help, I picked one, but we stipulated that the contract would not go into effect until I was eighteen. So, the first book was released the week after my birthday, but I got the bonus check on it. I was a published writer the day I became an adult. I have never done anything else," she finished, shrugging her shoulders.

"What did you do with the bonus?"

"I paid off Brian's house and the beach house. He had fallen behind on the payments on the beach house and was losing it. I made sure he got to keep it until he died," she said. She knew he hated that she had gotten the house in the will.

His eyebrows shot up. "That's why he left it to you?"

"No, he left it to me because I lived there. He left you his house in Tampa because you work in Tampa. He left us what we needed, not what we wanted," she replied, knowing his dad would have been upset with them fighting over the beach house.

During the story, she had dropped her computer onto her lap and she knew he could see her nipples pressing against the fabric of her shirt. She lifted the computer back up against her again, hugging it to her. She knew Zachary had no idea about Brian's finances. Brian would never have told him about it.

Silence filled the car again as the sign for Miami city limits came into view. At the first exit, he pulled the car off the highway for the first time all morning. They pulled into the parking lot of an all-night department store and stopped the car.

"What size do you want?"

"What?" she asked. What was he talking about?

"Shirt. What size, color?"

"I can go in," she argued.

"No, you're uncomfortable, so I'll get you something. I don't want to leave you out here, but I know you don't want to go in there. So, what size?" he repeated.

"Large," she whispered.

"Okay, see you in five. If you see something, go straight into that building, understand?" he said, his eyes locking with hers.

She nodded. His eyes were mesmerizing. Then he was gone. She watched him run across the parking lot and into the big box store. It wasn't a jog; it was a sprint.

Watching him, she wondered if his side was hurting him. He didn't indicate that it was. Though she had seen it when he opened the closet door, it wasn't until they were in the car that she looked more closely at it. It covered him from his armpit to midway down his stomach. Then across a few inches with a single wrap that went around his body.

When he had said he was shot, all she saw was Brian dying in that hospital bed from a gunshot to the chest. Now Zachary had been shot there, too, and it had scared her that she could have lost him from her life and that she wouldn't have known for days, maybe weeks, maybe ever.

Just as quickly as he ran in, she saw him running out. Though the distance was far, he wasn't winded when he climbed back in the car. His fly was all buttoned up now—she hadn't even noticed he had done it up. It was a little sad that she would not be able to see the peak of black underwear anymore.

Smiling, he handed her the bag. He seemed so proud of himself and his success in his mission. Looking in the bag, she pulled out a light blue sweatshirt. It was exactly what she wanted, except the color. She never wore blue. She slipped it over her head, and when she pulled her hair out from underneath it, she saw he was watching her. He quickly turned away, but not before she noticed the look of desire in his brown eyes. She had never seen that look on his face before, but she really liked it.

It wasn't until they got to the airport that she remembered she did not have her purse or her ID. There was no way she would be allowed on a plane.

"Zachary, I have no ID," she reminded him as he parked the car.

She watched as he pulled up his pants leg and pulled a gun out from a holster there. Sitting up, he said, "In the glove box."

Inside were three cards: two credit cards and her driver's license, except her name wasn't on any of them. "These are wrong, Zachary."

"For this week, honey, we are married. You are Zephyr Wainwright, and we are newlyweds," he replied, putting the gun in a case in the backseat.

Her mouth went dry as she looked at the three cards. Wainwright. Married. Married to Zachary.

"I-I don't know if it will work."

Zachary stopped and took her chin in his hand. "All marriages have problems, Zephyr. I think we can make ours work." Then he kissed the tip of her nose and got out of the car.

She sat there a moment, stunned, then pushed her way out of the car. "Not what I meant, Zachary. We don't get along."

"After last night, I plan on sticking closer to you then a husband would. It's only for a week, remember?" He lifted his bag out of the back seat.

"What about the credit cards? Are they fake?" she asked, following him. She clenched her computer to her chest while sliding the cards into the pocket of her sweatpants.

"Honey, those are real. We hooked them to your bank account," he answered as they walked across the sunny parking lot towards the building.

"I thought you talked to Ken yesterday about this. How did you get these done? Stop running! I can't keep up." It was only then that he slowed to a pace she could keep up with.

"I'm a cop. I have my ways." He put his arm around her shoulder.

"But that's what my real license looks like, except the name."

"It is as real as they come, honey. Now stop talking about it." He pulled her closer and whispered in her ear, "You're supposed to be in love with me."

It was on the tip of her tongue to say she was in love with him, but she bit it back and stuffed it deep inside her. That would never get out.

# CHAPTER SIX

THEY HAD BREEZED through security and check-in with one checked bag and one carry-on. Once they had sat on the plane, he was happy to find out Travis had booked them in first class. The seats were big and comfortable, but farther apart than they had been in the car for the last couple of hours. She felt miles from him instead of just a foot or so.

The moment she had sat down, she had put on her seatbelt and clutched that laptop. How long could she do that? But then again, every time she wasn't holding it in front of those glorious breasts, they were all his eyes could see. When she had pulled on the sweatshirt with her arms in the air, her shirt had ridden up enough that he saw a strip of skin between the top of her pants and the bottom of her shirt. His hands itched to touch the skin, then slide up to cup those beauties. Her nipples had made enough appearances that he wanted nothing but to see if they felt as good as they looked.

Before boarding, they had slipped into a gift shop and had bought snacks, and he had picked up a book for the trip. Every book she had released had been in the shop, and she hadn't even glanced at them. Maybe she didn't notice. Or did she not care?

"Are you going to write on the flight?"

"I don't know." She sat in the aisle but looked out the tiny window.

"Do you want me to put the computer in my bag?" he asked, pointing to his bag.

"No." She was still clenching the computer to her chest and looking past him out the window.

"You have to put it down when we take off," he informed her.

"When is that?" She was still looking out the window.

"Soon," he said, "Do you want to sit by the window?"

"No," she answered, still looking.

"Let's change." He stood up, and to his surprise, she got up too, and they switched places. "Computer?"

"Okay, here." She shoved it at him, then wrapped her arms around her stomach.

Sliding it into the bag, he looked at the back of her head. She was looking out the window again. Half her body was turned towards the window, and he noticed she was wearing a ring. He had never noticed she wore rings, but today, her thumb was spinning it with ease because it was too big for her.

"Who's ring?"

"My mom's. I thought I would leave it with them." She pulled her hand away from her and looked at the ring.

"Them?"

"Her girls." She moved her hand back so that she was hugging herself again.

He tilted his head in confusion. "Aren't you one of her girls?"

"No, they were her girls, a group I was not a part of." Her voice caught on the last words.

"Are you scared to fly?"

"I don't know. I have never done it," she admitted.

"How do you usually travel?" He wanted to know.

"I don't travel." She looked out the window.

"Never?"

"Never."

"Besides Florida, where have you been?"

She shrugged. "Nowhere. Just Florida."

"Georgia?" Everyone had been somewhere, why hadn't she been anywhere?

"Nope, just Florida."

"How did you promote your books?" he whispered, incredulous.

"I don't. That's why I have an editor and a publishing house." She still was turning away from him, looking out the window.

"Look at me," he said.

He was a little surprised when she actually looked at him. Her eyes were big blue orbs of fear. Taking both her hands in his, he put them together like she was praying and then held them both with one hand. With his free hand, he pushed a curl slowly behind her ear. Quietly he said, "It's going to be fine. I won't let anything happen to you."

The engines suddenly kicked in, and he felt her jump. As the plane started to move, he pulled her head towards his until their foreheads touched, and her eyes had nothing to look at but his. "I will take care of you. Will you let me take care of you?"

"Yes," she breathed out the word.

"You're just fine. I won't let anything happen to you," he whispered to her again as his hand slipped into her hair. He sighed when he felt the curls encase his hand, just like he had dreamed they would.

"I will take care of you. I will be here with you the entire time. Just relax." He held her and stared into her slowly blinking wide eyes. It took minutes for her to actually let her body relax. The plane had been in the air for a while before he saw she was smiling. Relaxed and smiling.

"I think I'm okay, Zachary. Thank you so much. I think I had a panic attack." With her words, he pulled his hand from her hair, dropping it onto his lap. Still, she kept her head resting against his.

"Glad I could help. That's what I do."

"Zachary," she whispered, and her blue eyes slid closed.

With a sigh, he moved to close the few inches between them and lightly touched her lips to his. Just once, just a light brush against her soft lips.

With all the strength he had, he pulled away from her soft,

glorious mouth. He would have given anything to pull her closer and deepen the kiss until his tongue was in her mouth, and she was moaning in his arms.

Cursing, he excused himself to the restroom. He didn't even check to see if he could get up, just got up and walked away. After closing the bathroom door, he leaned against it and cursed out loud. They hadn't even made it twelve hours into this, and he wanted to have sex with her on a plane.

It was supposed to be a hands-off week—no touching, definitely no kissing, and absolutely nothing more than that. She was almost his sister. His body didn't seem to care about who she could have been, just who she was now.

By the time he left the restroom, he had his mind and body under control. During his absence, she had pulled out her computer, but she wasn't typing. She had the screen pulled close to her and was staring at it.

"Did we lose your glasses?" He sat next to her.

Her eyes didn't leave the screen as she replied, "I don't wear glasses."

He looked over at her, and she was squinting at the screen in front of her. The screen was as close as she could get the laptop to her. Why was she lying to him? He had seen her in glasses hours before. She must have taken them off in the closet.

"Are you lying to me?" He called her on it.

She pushed the screen away and looked up at him. "I have the print small so that no one can read it. I have glasses for the glare when I type at night. I don't need glasses to see, close or far."

He watched as she clicked a series of keys and shut the computer. Pulling the USB drive from the socket, she handed it to him and said, "Put this in your pocket. I can't work anyway."

He took the small drive from her outstretched hand and slid it in his pocket, then took the computer from her lap and put it in the bag at his feet. Grabbing a pile of folders he had in his case, he handed them to her. He watched as she settled them on her lap, then straightened the pile and looked up at him.

"Those are files on the Hart girls and their spouses."

"I can see that by the labels ... because I don't need glasses." Her finger lightly touched each of the names. Then she sorted them by age, oldest to youngest.

"Did you want to know about them?"

"No," she whispered, staring at the neat pile on her lap.

"Have you ever looked them up on the internet?"

"No." She didn't move to open any of them, just looked at them on her lap.

"There are pictures in the files. Mostly driver's license pictures," he told her.

"Did you look at them?" she asked, looking up at him.

"Yes."

Her eyebrows raised in anticipation. "Do they look like me?"

"Yes."

"Who should I start with?"

"I thought you were going by age?" That was how she had sorted them.

She looked back down at the pile. "Is there a better way?"

He took them from her lap, trying his damnedest not to touch her. Resorting the files, he handed her Zoey's first. "This one. She could be your twin."

Zoey was six years older than Zephyr, though it was closer to seven, and Zoey was currently thirty. She had two kids and was married. Currently, she and their sister Evie ran a farm and sold vegetables and meat at farmer's markets.

Zephyr touched the name. "Mom loved her name. She always said Zoey was definitely a Zoey. That's how she said it. In a way, she named me Zephyr because she thought it sounded good with Zoey. Zoey and Zephyr. Sometimes she called her baby Zoey because she was so much younger than the other two. But I was way younger than them all, and she never called me baby."

Still, she didn't open the file. Instead, she just turned and looked out the window. "It's weird that I know so much about these women, but everything I know about them ended over twenty-three years ago.

They are still kids in my mind. Over the years, I grew up, but they never did. Suspended in time. When I open this, they become real, not just faded pictures."

"Do you want me to show you stuff? I can tell you and show you the pictures I have," he said, and she nodded, handing him back the files.

"Okay, this is my favorite picture I found of her. It was taken when she was still in the Army. She served for eight years. Enlisted while still in high school. I like this one because I can see you in it." He pulled out the picture of Zephyr's sister taken around the age Zephyr is now. If he had passed the woman on the street, he would have stopped her. She was the spitting image of his almost-sister.

As soon as he placed it on Zephyr's lap, he heard her gasp. Looking at her face, she looked like she had just seen a ghost. Or was she seeing herself in another life, based on different decisions? Except for the eyes, this was a picture of Zephyr in the Army.

"That was her then. This is a more recent picture. It's her driver's license picture, the most recent one." He handed the photo over.

Not as shocking as the last one. This picture showed a woman who was older than the last picture, but definitely the same person.

"She's thirty and married, has been for three years and has two kids. Her husband was a Marine before retiring and now is a cop. He is quite a bit older than her," he explained.

"I thought you said she was in the Army?"

"I did, and she was. He was Marines. His name is Gabriel Watson. They live on the farm the sisters were raised on," he said.

"Mom always said I looked like her. I guess she wasn't lying about that," Zephyr mussed.

He took the photos back and put them back in the file, then put it on the bottom of the pile. He only had one photo in the next file. "This one is Evangelina. She is thirty-four, married, and has three children. An older one from a previous marriage and two with her current husband, Jasper Reed. He grew up next door. She works with Zoey, and they farm. Before that, she farmed alone and with her father until his death."

"I have her eyes. Not the color, but the shape. Mom would always say that. She didn't know where the blue came from. I guess she never thought of the man as anything; no genes could come from him." She chuckled at her joke.

He watched her looking down at the photo and chuckled as well. "I think she might have been right. The sperm donor didn't give you four much." He pulled out the last picture and let it fall onto her lap.

"Della. She looks like Mom, just like Mom. This is how I remember Mom looking. Mom was never this elegant, but she's right there."

Zachary looked at the photo she held. "That, Zephyr, is your oldest sister. She is thirty-six years old now. She is married and has two children. Both are adopted. She lives in the house that your mom was raised in. A few years ago, she started a law firm and ran it out of the house. There are still lawyers at Hart Law Firm, but she doesn't work there anymore."

"Where did she go?" Zephyr asked, worry thick in her voice.

"Nowhere. She is now Judge Delphinea Connor Hart. She was elected judge a few years ago," he said and smiled at the shock on her face. He had been just as surprised about her sisters' accomplishments.

"Can I have Zoey's picture back?"

Handing her the picture, he watched her compare each to the other and then back to another. A few minutes into the comparing, she pulled out her driver's license from her pocket. She started to compare herself to them.

"Zachary, I won't be able to not tell them who I am. They will notice me right away. I look just like them. I don't know if I want them to know about me. I just want to see them ... see if they are like her."

"Her being your mom?"

She nodded. "Yes, or him."

"Him being her husband?" His heart hurt for the girl who had been rejected by so many people.

"Yes, them. I don't what to know them if they are."

"Based on all I have read and learned, they are nothing like them, but I do understand. I was thinking a change in hairdo. Straight with a different color. We can't change that you're as short as them," he said. At the last remark, she stuck her tongue out at him, and he laughed. "You, my dear wife, are the second tallest of the sisters … unless they lied on their licenses."

"They're short too? What about these?" She squeezed her breast together from the sides.

Laughing at her, he said, "Driver's licenses do not disclose cup size."

"They should." She went back to looking at the pictures.

"Do you want the files?" He offered her the pile.

He liked that she took them and could open them right away this time. The information was basic, but it was more than she had ever had. Over her shoulder, he watched her reading. She read quickly, flipping through pages so fast he was convinced she didn't read them. But every once in a while, she would ask a question.

As they neared their destination, they hit turbulence, and she grabbed his hand tightly. After that, she used only one hand to flip through the papers and pictures. Sometimes she used their hands together to move something or nudge something, but she never let it go. Her hold loosened from the death grip to something softer over time.

Enjoying the remaining time on the flight, he watched her shuffle through the papers and pictures, her small hand in his the entire time. It was warm and soft and so pale compared to his darker skin. Staring at where their hands were laced together, the contrast of their skin mesmerized him. He let his mind run around the feelings of her hand in his and the sight of it. It wasn't that he had never dated or even had sex with white women, but there was something different about Zephyr. Zephyr was always different.

He drifted off to sleep, knowing she was safe right next to him on the plane. They were even holding hands. She couldn't get away if she tried.

# CHAPTER SEVEN

WHEN THE PLANE LANDED, Zephyr wasn't as scared as when it took off. It helped that she was holding Zachary's strong hand. It helped that she was looking out the window in hopes of seeing snow. There was none. It also helped that Zachary was still asleep, and when she stopped looking for snow, she could look at his relaxed face.

He had been sleeping for around an hour, and she knew he was tired. They had been up for almost twelve hours and had covered a lot of miles in that time, and they would cover even more. There was no way this guy could still be following them.

As the plane taxied, she carefully put the papers back in their files. The first time she had looked through them, she had looked for herself in each one. She could see the mom they shared in each one, and she had seen herself in each one.

Did she see people she wanted to spend time with or sisters who would accept her? She couldn't say. They seemed nice enough on paper.

For the first time, she wondered if their father had told them about her. Maybe they knew the entire time and didn't need another sister in their lives. Maybe they didn't care what had happened to their mother.

As the plane came to a stop, Zephyr looked over at Zachary, still sleeping next to her. Staring at his mouth, she remembered the soft kiss he had given her. Had she dreamed it, or had it happened? By the time her eyes opened, he was gone, walking away from her towards the restroom.

When he had come back, he had said nothing to her about it. Maybe it was just her imagination. It was a pretty wild one sometimes, but never had her thinking she had kissed a man that she may not have.

"Zachary," she whispered in his ear. His eyes popped open at his name. She had thought he would be groggy, but he was on high alert for a moment until he relaxed against the seat.

"Did I fall asleep?"

"Yep. The plane has landed. You slept for quite a while," she explained. Handing him the folders, she watched as he slid them into the bag at his feet, then slid the zipper closed on it.

When the passengers could leave, he stood up, grabbed his bag with his free hand, and threw it over his shoulder. Her hand never left his as they got off the plane and walked into another airport, thousands of miles from the last one they were in.

After gathering their checked bag, they made it to the car rental office. Zachary talked to the man behind the counter as Zephyr looked out the window at fall in Minnesota. It was nothing great.

Zachary waved her over, and they walked into the cold fall day. The sun was shining, but it was not putting out any heat. Cold was cold here, whereas, in Florida, cold was chilly. Zachary had dropped her hand when he'd grabbed his duffle bag off the conveyer. Now running across the parking lot, he took her hand again as he pulled her towards a line of cars.

Once they'd stopped, he pointed at one that was bigger than any car she had ever owned. She knew it was an SUV, but that was all she knew. Nodding, she went to the passenger door and opened it. After sliding in, she immediately decided it was the nicest car she had ever ridden in.

Zachary threw their stuff in the back, then slid into the driver's door and smiled at her. "Welcome to Minnesota, Zephyr Hart." Then he started the vehicle and quickly strapped a gun to his leg.

Before she knew it, they had maneuvered their way out of the parking lot and were on the interstate heading out of town. Not much was different from Tampa, maybe the trees and grass, but the buildings were the same.

"Do you miss your cell phone? It was left at your house, wasn't it?" Zachary asked as he drove.

Turning to the man quizzically, she stated, "I don't have a cell phone."

"How do you *not* have a cell phone? Everyone has a cell phone," he asked incredulously.

"I have a landline, and that's all I need. Nobody calls." Nobody did call. Her editor did every once in a while, maybe.

"How do you keep up with all your internet stuff?"

"I don't have any."

"I saw it! You're all over."

She shrugged. "The publishing company takes care of that stuff. I just write."

"Do you want one?"

"No need. Nobody calls, anyway," she said. Having to say it so many times, it bothered her a little that nobody called.

"I would call you," he said.

"Call my landline. I'm usually home." She smiled at him.

He smiled back. "Are you ready to shop, Mrs. Wainwright?"

"I'm ready to not be in sweats," she admitted. Zephyr hated shopping—she was no good at it. Her formative years were spent being broke, so spending money now was still hard.

Soon, they were pulling into a parking lot at a strip mall. There were stores that sold everything here. Clothing, jewelry, shoes, everything.

"What do you need?" he asked.

"I need a power cord for my computer and headphones," she answered with the first thing that came to mind.

"Focus, Zephyr. Clothes first," he said.

"Clothes then," she replied with a sigh. He followed her and pointed out a few stores, but the one closest to the car seemed to be the best choice. And it would get them out of the cold fastest.

Together they walked into the store, and a saleswoman walked up to them immediately, asking if they needed help. Zephyr wanted to crawl into a hole since the woman was wearing perfectly tailored clothes, and she was in sweatpants and sandals.

"My wife needs new clothes," Zachary said matter-of-factly. "Seven days' worth of new clothes."

The woman turned to Zephyr and grinned. "You came to the right place. Let's see what we can find. I'm Paige."

"I'm Zephyr."

"What a unique name. Pretty," Paige answered with a nod.

"Thank you. It's just weird," Zephyr stated her usual answer when people found out her name.

"So, you need seven days of clothes? What kind?" Page asked as Zachary hung back.

"My husband has surprised me with a trip up north for seven days. Surprise means he didn't let me pack anything." Most of it was true.

"Lake country?" Paige questioned

"Yes." Zephyr went with it, wherever that was.

"How romantic." Paige looked at Zachary, who was looking at his phone near the front of the building.

"It is. Just a little inconvenient." She smiled.

"Oh, sweetie, it is very inconvenient. What do you usually wear?"

Zephyr looked down at her frumpy outfit. Oddly, it was mostly this. "Shorts or jeans and T-shirts, mostly. But I want something different."

Paige laughed at her. "No shorts this week. How about we look over here?"

The woman walked around the store, picking out outfits and folding them over her arm. Zephyr followed behind, wondering how she could just put together outfits. Did the woman know it would all look good together, or was she guessing? Zephyr could describe color at length for pages, but matching a top and pants? No way. Coordinating colors was not something Zephyr could do.

When the other woman's arms were full, she led Zephyr to the back of the store where the dressing rooms were. Paige set the pile in a chair just outside the room and started sorting them, making outfits from the pieces. Once she got one together, she put it in a dressing room.

"Try this one on and see how it looks." Paige held open the door for her.

"Okay, but do you have any undergarments in the store?" Zephyr questioned, biting her lip. This was so embarrassing.

"Yes, we do," Paige said and then looked at Zephyr's chest. "But nothing that will fit you."

"Okay. I just don't have a bra on right now," Zephyr mumbled, hoping that would explain everything.

She could tell Paige was trying to find a solution. Then her face brightened, and she said, "Come with me." She grabbed her hand and headed for the front door. She called to the other lady in the store, "I'm taking lunch."

As she was being pulled from the store, she looked for Zachary, but he was nowhere to be seen. So, she just followed the woman down four storefronts and let herself be pulled into the fifth. When the door opened, it was full of bras, panties, and socks. Paige called out to one of the employees behind the counter, "Bridget, we have an emergency!"

The blonde woman behind the counter came rushing to them. "What?"

Paige explained, "Her gorgeous romantic husband has whisked her away for a romantic week up north, but he didn't let her pack anything. *Anything.*"

"A week? How long have you been married?" Bridget asked.

"Not long." Zephyr didn't lie.

"So, you're thinking seven panties and seven bras?" Bridget asked Paige.

"Yes, and something comfortable and pretty. He's gorgeous."

Both women turned to her, and Bridget asked, "What size are you?"

Paige looked at her and said, "She's got a rack under there."

"I don't really know what size they are. I usually wear sports bras. Others just hurt most of the time," Zephyr admitted to the two women.

"Not here. I will not sell you something that doesn't work for you. Let's go measure, and then we will find the right bra," Bridget replied happily, pulling her back to the dressing rooms in the back of the store.

Once her measurements were taken, Bridget slipped out, leaving Zephyr half-naked in a strip mall in a town she had never heard of before. It felt weird, new weird. Bridget's hand suddenly slipped back into the room, holding a lacy lavender bra. Grabbing it from her, Zephyr put it on. It fit perfectly. In her entire life, she had never had a bra that fit. This one did.

Leaving it on, she pulled the tag off and put her sweatshirt back on. Zephyr grabbed the T-shirt with her when she left the room, throwing it away when she found a garbage can. She said, "A few more of those, please."

The two ladies cheered, then Paige said, "And matching panties for all. All colors."

Once they were all in the bag, Zephyr pulled out her credit card. *Let's see if this works*, she thought. When the transaction went through, she almost cheered as well. She had money! Once she had paid for her purchases and left a generous tip, she and Paige rushed back to the clothing store.

When they got there, she could see right away Zachary was mad at her. Stalking over to her as they rushed in, he pushed her into a corner. Lowering his head close to her ear, he whispered harshly, "Where were you?"

"Paige took me to another store," she said, eyeing her new friend, who was looking at them, concerned.

"Do you know what could have happened to you?" he whispered, but he ran his fingers gently across her cheek as he said it.

"I am fine. See?" She pushed him away.

Walking away from him without looking back, Zephyr held her head high and sauntered into the dressing room to try on the outfits. Once she got the brown pants and off-white sweater on, she saw right away that the combination was amazing. It even made her hair seem less red. When she stepped out to show Paige, the only person she saw was Zachary. His eyes raked her body from head to toe. His expression was unreadable, but Paige squealed with delight at the outfit.

"Do you like it?" Page asked.

"Yes, it's very comfortable, but it doesn't look comfortable; it looks sophisticated. But the shirt is a bit itchy," Zephyr said, tearing her eyes from Zachary to look at Paige.

"Easy fix. We'll add a tank top for that one—less itchy that way," Paige replied.

"I have another outfit in this one." Paige pushed Zephyr into the next dressing room. "But if you like it, don't come out. I don't want brown eyes over there to see all your outfits. Leave a little surprise."

"Brown eyes watches everything." Zephyr giggled.

It took over an hour in the store with Paige to get all the outfits she needed for the week. Zephyr also needed some clothes she could write in, so Paige brought up some nice, soft stretchy pants that were not sweatpants, and a few nice comfy tops to go with them. A pair of brown boots were added to the pile since sandals were not good enough for this late in the fall. Taking the piles of clothes to the register, it took time to ring up the total.

Zephyr had decided to wear something new out of the store, choosing white pants and a soft gray sweater from the pile. She threw the sweatpants in the garbage but had them put the sweatshirt in the bag. Even though the color was wrong on her, Zachary had bought it for her. She noticed the entire pile was earth tones, so now she had a color pallet that worked for her.

Paige gave her a total that had crested the four-digit mark. With a smile, she slid her card through the machine. Money well-spent. Paige handed her the receipt to sign and added a tip that matched the original total.

"I cannot accept this, Zephyr. It's too much," Paige protested.

"No, it's not. You are great at your job. I wish I had met you years ago. Treat your kids to something special. Do you know a hairdresser I could get into at the last minute?" Zephyr brushed off the woman's complaints.

"Yes, three doors down. I will make sure Patty has time for you," Paige assured her with a gentle smile.

Before Zephyr left the shop, both ladies gave her a hug and told her not to color her hair. They would hunt her down if she did. The hair salon was near the car, so Zachary stepped away to put the bags in the car while she went into the shop. He would keep an eye on her from there.

True to Paige's word, Patty had the chair ready for her when she walked in. Patty was a middle-aged woman with spiky pink hair and a huge smile. "What can I do for you, honey?"

"I need the curls gone, and the color changed," Zephyr said as she sat down.

Spinning her in the chair, Patty ran her fingers through the riot of curls. "Is this all natural?"

"This is how it looks all the time."

"I constantly have women in here wanting this. I can't give women this hair," Patty said in wonder.

"I need a change. I look a lot like my sisters, and I am ready to be different." Zephyr told the truth.

"Let's straighten it and cut it and see if that is enough," Patty replied, nodding her head.

Just as Patty was starting to trim away at her long curls, Zachary poked his head in and said, "I'm going into the store next door and getting a suitcase. Do you want a wallet or purse?"

"Wallet," she called out to him.

"You know what to do," he called back as he left her.

"He's good-looking. Kind of pushy, though."

"You get used to it," Zephyr said. It was true, but she knew why he was acting the way he was. Still, she wished he would relax a little.

Patty was easy to talk to. She had Zephyr expanding on the story of her and Zachary. It was a good thing her imagination was more than up to the task. Patty wanted details about how they met, the wedding, dates. By the time the older woman had straightened, cut, and styled her hair, Zephyr noticed that Zachary was sitting in the waiting area, reading a book. Was he listening? Probably. He had to be able to hear them.

Spinning the chair to face the mirror, Patty said, "How does that look? Enough of a change?"

Staring out from the mirror was a woman Zephyr had never seen before. Her hair was styled in a sleek bob that grazed her shoulders. It looked darker than it had ever looked, more auburn than the red she always thought it was.

"Will the curls come back?" She touched the straight hair.

"Yes. You'll have to get it straightened once a month to keep it straight."

"What if it curls when it is wet?"

"It shouldn't. If so, I have a straightener you can buy."

"I actually need everything that made this possible. I have nothing with me," Zephyr replied, eyes going wide.

Standing up, she called out to Zachary, who was not watching her for the first time since he showed up on the beach. When his eyes raised to hers, that guarded expression was gone for a heartbeat, and his eyes darkened with desire. Desire for her.

"Do you like it?" she asked when his guard was back up.

"You look gorgeous, Zephyr. You always are, but this is amazing." He got up and looked at her from head to toe. Everything had changed in the last few hours.

Smiling at him, she turned to the hairdresser and said, "I need everything you used on the hair."

Patty happily gathered up all the items she had used and put them in a bag for Zephyr. Ringing up the total, Zephyr realized this trip was going to cost more than she spent on clothing and her hair in a year or maybe three. But it was worth it.

Again, the receipt came, and she gave the older woman a nice-sized tip. The hairdresser argued about the money but eventually accepted it. Another hug, and Zephyr was out the door. Zachary led her to the car, but she protested. "I need a cord for my computer. And headphones."

Zachary scanned the stores and saw one that the end of the row. "Get in. We'll drive. I'll run in and get them. You'd buy everything in the store if I let you go in."

Pulling into a spot close to the store, he added, "Stay in here. If you see anything, run towards the store."

"Okay. Can I have my USB drive back?" she asked.

He dug in his pocket and handed it to her, then was out of the car and into the store. Zephyr watched him as he went. While he was gone, she slid the USB drive into her bra. Then she filled her wallet, which didn't take any time.

True to his word, he was out of the store quicker than she would have thought possible. He handed her the bag, and she looked inside. Two cords and a large pair of headphones. "Thanks, Zachary. Now I can work anywhere."

"Just not in the closet anymore. Why were you in the closet last night?" He started the car.

"Because you're a light sleeper. I didn't want to wake you," she admitted.

"You were in another room with the door closed. I'm not *that* light of a sleeper."

"I guess I was just being stupid." She looked out the window.

The town started to fall away, and the countryside opened up in the twilight. Now the differences between Florida and Minnesota were stark; there were no leaves on the trees, and the grass was turning brown in the lawns. Zephyr was used to it being humid and warm, but this was cold and dry. She could feel the harshness of the landscape. Every plant was dying before her eyes. Some would come back one day, but some were gone forever.

Black field after black field met her eyes. Watching each one disappear into the distance, she wanted to ask Zachary to stop so she could get out, but he was mad now, and she didn't want to make him even madder. So, she dreamed she could get out and walk and touch, maybe smell it. From her comfortable seat, she knew it would smell different.

"Zephyr, you are not stupid. Don't call yourself that. You were in there because you are the most considerate person I know. You sat in a closet in your own home to work, just so you wouldn't wake me. But for this trip, no more closets, okay?" His voice was softer as he asked.

"Okay," she said as she watched the colors fall away while the sun dipped over the horizon.

Could it have possibly been only yesterday that she had watched him watch the sunset? So much had happened since then; so many miles had been traveled. But the sun was setting for them again, with all its glorious color.

She fought the urge to lean over to him and say, "Hell of a day it's been." But his mind was elsewhere now. He had been silent for a while. What was he thinking? Was he mad that he was here with her? Was he upset that he had to protect her? Did he still hate her after all these years? Would it be possible that one day, he wouldn't hate her and that they could be friends?

The car was in complete darkness now, with the only light coming from the dash. The blue light made Zephyr feel lonely, and his silence wasn't helping.

Breaking the silence, he said, "You shouldn't tip so much, Zephyr."

"It's my money. I can use it like I want to," she reminded him.

"I know it's your money, but you can't just throw it around. It isn't going to last if you keep it up." He did not look at her.

She raised an eyebrow at him. "Do you know how many books I've sold?"

"No, but I do know you have pre-sold a lot for the next one coming. If that's just the presale, you've sold a lot. But that's not the point. People will take advantage of you," Zachary insisted.

"I make over two dollars a book, every book. First running, I get more. I get more money for an advance on a book than you make in a year, maybe even two. I have the money, and I like to share it. It makes me feel good to give it away. I don't need it all," she said confidently.

"Then give it to a charity. You don't know how these people will spend it. What if they just blow it on booze and drugs?" he asked.

"I guess they'll spend it on whatever. I don't give it and say it must be spent this way or that."

"Why do you really do it, Zephyr?"

"When I was a kid, I remember Mom coming home from work all excited. Someone had tipped her one hundred dollars, and she was so excited. We didn't have money floating around ever. She walked in the door and said, 'Zeph, we are going out on the town. Tonight, we are queens of this city. Steak for all.' In my mind, these women are going home tonight, excited at their good fortune. And it really cost me nothing," she said into the darkness between them.

"Is that why you don't want anyone to call you, Zeph? Because your mom did?" he asked.

"When she was happy, she called me that. Usually, she called me Zephyr. She wasn't happy all that often," she admitted.

"Life had dealt her a difficult hand," he agreed.

"And I am the worst card she ever got," she whispered.

"She didn't think that, Zephyr. She loved you." He reached out and put his hand on her shoulder.

"When she was drunk, she would tell me I was her biggest mistake. I was the reason she was in Florida, and the kids she loved were not with her."

"She didn't mean it."

"I lived in the shadows of these girls for twelve years. I just hope they live up to it," she replied, clamping back the tears from the memories of days past.

The hand that was once on her shoulder was now resting on the nape of her neck, under her now-straight hair. His fingers were lazily rubbing the side of her neck. Zephyr stayed perfectly still, knowing he would pull away if she leaned into the touch.

"Do you remember your parents?" she asked to get the conversation off her. She had never asked him about his past before Brian adopted him.

"Not really. They were already dead when I was six. Dad first in a car accident, he was pretty high when it happened. Years ago, I read the file on it, and it was his fault. He hit a tree going close to eighty miles an hour. I don't remember him. I was around two. Then Mom took me and left Jacksonville and moved to the beach. We had a little apartment near a park, but the drugs found us there, too. She was high most days, usually too high to feed me. Sometimes a neighbor would feed me, but mostly, I ate only at school. All I remember is being hungry all the time." He stopped talking and turned off the interstate as the voice on his phone told him to do.

"When I was six, she overdosed while I was at school. I came home and found her. By that time, we were living in a dive apartment. The landlord called the cops. One of the cops was Brian, and within a month, he had adopted me. After that, I had it pretty good. At the time, you couldn't have told me that. I was a jerk kid sometimes. But through it all, Brian loved me," he finished, and the car went silent again. The road was narrower now, and the cars coming towards them were fewer.

"Brian was the one that told me about my mom. He was really good with kids. Do you know why he never married or had kids of his own?" she asked.

"No, he never said."

"To me, either," she whispered, his hand was still resting on the nape of her neck, but his pinky had slid under her shirt and was caressing her back. The touch was nothing intimate, but Zephyr felt the tingle and sparks that it caused coursing through her body. *Just a week. Get through this week without embarrassing yourself,* was her only thought.

# CHAPTER EIGHT

HER SKIN WAS SO warm and soft, and he couldn't stop his hand from touching it. He'd tried. But here on the dark, lonely road, he let go and caressed the pale skin he had wanted to touch all day. It felt better than he had ever dreamed it would.

It had been the quiet comfort of the car that had made him talk about his past. Or was it the comforting way Zephyr talked? Her story about her mom had broken his heart and made him hate the woman just a little bit more. Every time she talked about her mother, there were good times tinged with sadness. The only reason that Zephyr had never sought out her sisters was because of her mom. Her mom had spent years making Zephyr guilty for being there when her sisters were not. Guilty that it had been her fault the woman had never gone back to her other kids. So much of her mother's talking about Zephyr had been in comparison to the kids she loved and lost that Zephyr didn't get to feel loved or wanted.

As his hand brushed the nape of her neck, he missed the curls grabbing at his fingers. When he had seen her walking towards him in the hair salon, he had been rendered speechless; tongue-tied like a teenager. She had started the trip as a young woman who preferred frumpy, comfortable clothes, and he was having a hard time keeping his hands off her. The woman who walked towards him was a sleek and stylish version of Zephyr. There were curves that had been hidden under the sweatpants and T-shirts, and he had wanted to pull her into his arms and kiss her. Or run his hands through the sleek hair or maybe just around her waist where her white pants met the gray sweater. He wanted to run his hands under the sweater until he felt soft skin beneath his fingers.

Thankfully, all he did was stare. Maybe a little too rudely, but he couldn't take his eyes off her transformation. He started to worry that he was going to look drab compared to the woman in front of him.

When Zephyr had first gone off with Paige, he had purchased a few sweaters and long-sleeve shirts from the other saleswoman. He had run them out to the car, and when he had gotten back, she was gone. He had frantically searched the store and the street outside. Back inside, he searched the dressing rooms and the bathroom. She was gone. His heart was pounding—he had lost her. Had she been kidnapped?

His mind was racing with all the possibilities when she had calmly walked back into the store, just as cool as could be. As he pushed her into the corner of the store, he knew he was overreacting, and she didn't need to be treated like a child. The relief washed through him as he held her by the waist. She was safe, and she was back.

After that, he stuck close by, maybe to close sometimes. When she had walked out of the dressing room in the white sweater, desire for her overtook him, but he slammed it down. He was sure she saw it, though. Their eyes had been glued to each other.

When she wore clothes that didn't cover her body like a blanket, she was all curves. All he wanted to do was pull her to him and touch her.

Clearing his throat and pushing those thoughts away, he said, "We were supposed to be there hours ago."

"Where?" she asked.

"I booked us in a B&B in Birch Cove," he explained.

"Doesn't one of the husbands have a B&B?"

He could tell she was on to him. Once he had seen that information, he knew exactly where they would be staying. No reason to stay at a hotel when they could stay right with the people they had come to see.

"Yes, and that's the one."

"No, Zachary, it's too close," she said and dropped her head to look at her lap. Taking full advantage, he spread his fingers wide to touch as much of the exposed skin as possible.

"If we are going to run into them, we better be underfoot. It will be fine. But we're late." He tried to calm her.

Reluctantly, he pulled his hand away from her neck and put it on the steering wheel again. They were pulling into town, and he needed to make a turn soon. The highway that they had been driving on turned into Main Street. Halfway through the town, the road he needed came up. Turning, he knew the house was only a block away.

Parking outside the dark Bed and Breakfast, he shut off the engine. It wasn't the old Victorian that caught their attention; it was the house across the street. Most of the lights were on and cast light out of the windows. It was huge, and the reports had called it a mansion, and it was a correct assessment. It was giant. Both he and Zephyr got out of the car, and their eyes didn't leave the house.

Walking around the car, Zachary took her hand in his. "We have to check-in at the law office." He pointed at the sign in the lawn in front of the huge house that said Hart Law Firm.

As they headed for the house, she was at first reluctant, but then went easy with him as they walked. He wondered if she thought this was the house her mother had been raised in, so very different from the places she herself had been raised in.

When they stopped on the front porch, he turned to her and pulled her into his arms for a comforting hug. The warmth that came off her body felt good in the cold darkness.

"We can walk away right now. We don't have to do this." He meant it. They had come thousands of miles and spent a lot of money, but if she wanted to leave, he would walk her back to the car.

"No, you're right. I have to do this. I have to put these people behind me," she said, and he saw she was smiling. She pulled him tighter into the hug and rested her head against his shoulder for a moment before pulling away.

"Okay." He rang the doorbell.

They could hear the bell ring inside the large house. Squeezing her hand, he smiled down at her when she looked up at him. With her makeover, she did not look as much like the sisters as she had before. Taming the curls that they all sported was a big part of it. With the straight hair, the other features that were so recognizable were dulled.

It took time, but the big door finally opened. Turning, they saw a tall man in jeans and a sweatshirt, dark hair, and a big smile. "I thought you guys got lost. The Wainwrights, correct?"

"Yes," Zachary answered the man. "Zachary, and my wife, Zephyr."

"Max Valentine. Come in a second. I have to grab shoes and the key." Max stepped back and let them inside the beautiful house.

The woodwork and hardwood floors were shiny and stunning. The main floor was set up as office space with desks and chairs, but a grand staircase dominated the main floor. Max was sitting on the bottom step, tying his shoes.

"It is beautiful, isn't it? I married my wife so I could live here," he said with a laugh. Then he yelled up the stairs. "Isn't that right, Dell? I married you for your house."

Zachary turned to see Zephyr's face over the exchange. Her expression had him pulling her a little closer. Was it the house where her mother was raised, or the fact that her sister was upstairs? Either one could have been the cause, but Zephyr was white as a ghost. He put his arm around her shoulder.

The voice from upstairs called, "You married me because you couldn't keep your hands off me, Max Valentine."

In Zachary's mind, the words echoed off the walls, echoing into his mind. Until that moment, he had never thought that Zephyr's voice was anything special. Now he had heard it without a slight southern accent, an accent he had never heard in her voice. He made a note not to let her talk on the phone to these people ... she had her sister's tone.

Max had gotten his last shoe on and laughed at his wife's words. "She's right. I can't."

"So, you guys are from Florida. What brings you up to Minnesota?" he asked as he looked through a box hanging on the wall.

"Family," Zachary answered.

"Snow," Zephyr said at the same time.

"I hope we don't see any until after Halloween, but we're supposed to get snow on Wednesday, so maybe you'll see some. I would ask about the family, but I have only lived here for a few years and don't know a lot of people." Max was completely relaxed with strangers in his house.

Max found the key and turned to them. Zachary still had his arm around Zephyr's shoulder. "Are you okay, Mrs. Wainwright? You look pale."

Zephyr straightened her back. "I'm fine. just a long day."

"You look familiar. Do you have family here or your husband?"

Zachary jumped in with the answer. "I do."

He wondered what Max thought about Zachary being the one with family in town. How many black families were there in this small Minnesota town? Did he think it odd the black man had the relative and not the pale white woman? Max showed no indication of what he was thinking, just went to the door and walked out of the big house.

Zachary and Zephyr followed him across the street to the other house. On the front porch, Max put the key in the lock and said, "This was my great aunt's house. She died a few years ago and left me the place. I can't make myself sell it, but I also don't want to live here. I like it over there."

Max quickly had the door open and was turning on the lights in the house. It was not as beautiful as the one they were just at, but it had its own charm. The furniture was old but not worn, a little more formal than Zachary would ever choose, but it fit the house perfectly.

"You guys are here alone as we don't have any other guests so far. I'll leave the key on the table by the door. If you go out, lock up," Max explained.

"Are you a lawyer?" Zachary asked. It seemed odd asking since everyone in the room knew the answer.

"Yes and no. I was a lawyer once, but now I write books. I enjoy that a lot more," Max said.

"What kind of books?" Zephyr perked up at the information.

It was the only thing she had said except for 'snow.' Zachary watched the older man's face to see if he recognized his wife's voice coming from another woman, but it seemed Max didn't notice at all.

"Historical. My first was about the mob, but lately, I have been working on the history of this town. It has been very interesting. What do you two do?" Max asked.

The two looked at each other—they had not talked about this at all. Zachary answered, "I'm in real estate, and she's getting her doctorate."

"Wow. Do not tell my wife; she dreams of a doctorate. In what?" Max looked at her.

Again, Zachary answered, "Creative writing."

"Good luck, but if you've made it this far, you don't need luck. You don't look old enough to have made it through that much school," Max observed.

"She's smarter than she lets on. Maybe young but has put in the work." He pulled her into a side hug.

"I've got one of those as well. She's a judge and whines about not getting a doctorate. A judge by thirty-five, but still she complains," Max said as he led them up the stairs.

"This one will probably be like that in ten years, too," Zachary replied.

"Twelve." Zephyr quietly corrected him. Della was twelve years older than she was.

"I've put you in the turret room since it's one of the bigger ones and is close to the bathroom. If you want to change to another, that is fine." Max opened the door to the decent-sized room. The bed was in the middle of the floor, but there was enough room for a large comfy chair and a desk.

"It's very nice. I think it will work for us," Zachary said.

When Zachary turned from surveying the room, he saw Max was staring at Zephyr, who wasn't noticing the attention. Zachary wondered if the man had seen something that would connect the dots. Max must have noticed Zachary was staring at him.

"Are you sure you don't have any relatives around here, Mrs. Wainwright?" Max asked again.

"You can call me, Zephyr. No, I have never even been to Minnesota before." He had noticed she never really lied, just talked around the answer—her doctorate in creative writing in action.

"I'm sorry. I guess it's just because my wife comes from a family of redheads. The Hart family is known for their red hair," Max explained.

"Is your wife a redhead?" Zephyr avoided his explanation.

"Yes, but hers is curly. She's short like you, though," Max explained.

"Well, we should get our bags, honey." Zachary broke up the discussion.

Max stopped looking at Zephyr. "Yes, I will be over to make breakfast in the morning around seven or eight. Is that okay?"

"You, not your wife?" Zephyr was unaware of the scrutiny.

"Me. This is my baby, so she doesn't help me with it unless she wants to." He grinned.

"Oh." Zephyr followed him down the hallway.

Once Max was gone, Zachary started to bring in the luggage. For them having nothing a few hours ago, they suddenly had more than he could take into the house in three trips. While he was taking in the bags, he surveyed the neighborhood for something strange or out of place. Nothing caught his eye. When he made it to the room with the last of the loads, Zephyr was putting things away like she lived here. Hair stuff went in the bathroom, and then she went back to putting clothes in the empty dresser.

Sitting on the bed, he watched her fold her new clothes and place them into the drawers. Each outfit got a half of a drawer. Her movements were slow and mesmerizing, and soon, his eyes were wandering. He should put his own stuff away, but his body was too heavy to make it do that. He had been up too long today.

# CHAPTER NINE

INSTANTLY, he was awake. Instantly, he was on alert. Instantly, he grabbed the person in front of him to subdue them. Get the intruder subdued, think later. He flipped them on the bed and rolled onto them to pin their legs. Get their hands above their head. All done with no thinking involved.

Then his mind cleared, and he started thinking and feeling again. Zephyr's body wiggled under his, and her breasts pressed into his chest. He could feel Zephyr's heat pressing against his erection and her small hands in his. Zephyr's breath came, stopped, then started again with a deep breath.

Lifting his head to see her face, his eyes locked on hers, and he watched her face break out in a smile. She started laughing. Her body shook under his with laughter. Rolling off her, he lay on his back and joined in with her. They lay side by side, laughing for minutes.

"That was interesting."

"Sorry, you took me by surprise," he said.

Sitting up, he noticed she had changed into a white T-shirt and had nothing else on. When she noticed he was looking at her, she crossed her arms over her chest and said, "It's yours, but I forgot to get something to sleep in. And none of my new shirts cover my butt."

He smiled at her. "It looks better on you." *What an old line*, he thought.

"Okay," she said suspiciously. "Now, how are we going to sleep? We have the entire house."

Sitting up, he rubbed his head and replied, "We should stay in one room. I can't protect you if you're somewhere else."

He watched as she looked around the room. There was plenty of space, but the only other place to sleep was the floor. "Are we going to take turns on the floor then?"

"No, I think the bed is big enough for us both. I think we can be adults about this and sleep together," he said, shaking his head.

Getting up, he emptied the pockets of his jeans and then took the gun off his leg and placed it on the nightstand. Next, he pulled off his shirt and threw it on the chair. She was crawling into the bed, tucking those glorious legs under the covers. And he had just gotten to see them.

"I thought that doing what adults do in bed was off the table?" she asked.

He turned to her as he undid his belt. "Did I say that?" He tried to remember if they had talked about sex. He would have remembered talking about sex with her.

"No, I guess it was implied," she said more to herself. She was blushing.

"It is. You don't have to worry that something will happen."

"Okay." She turned over so that she was lying on her side.

Where did this come from? What was she talking about? Grabbing his bag, he went into the bathroom to get ready for bed. By the time he came out of the bathroom, she looked to be sleeping. Glancing at his phone, he saw it was only nine, but with the time change and the long day, he was as ready as her to sleep. He shut the lights off as he walked into the room, finding his way around by the light from the streetlight outside. He slid out of his jeans and climbed into bed. Even though she was across the bed from him, he could feel her heat and wanted to pull her closer. Instead, he flopped on his back and looked at the ceiling.

He heard Zephyr sigh in the dark and wondered if she was really sleeping. They had talked more today than they had in the last ten years. By the time they had made it out of Tampa, he had seen the person Brian had seen. She was fun and easy to talk to. She was the most honest and generous person he had met in a long time. The pain she carried with her from childhood was just below the surface. If you scratched it, she would bleed.

With any luck, they would be able to meet all the sisters over the next few days, and then they could move on. He had no idea where to go next, maybe out west. For some reason, he was starting to think that if they kept moving, this guy would not be able to find them. And if she was still in danger after this week, there was no way she was getting rid of him.

"Do you think Max recognized me?" she asked into the dark. He had thought she was sleeping.

"I think if he had known there was another sister out there, he would have pegged you once you opened your mouth," he said to the ceiling.

He felt her roll onto her back. "What did I say wrong?"

"Nothing, but you sound exactly like his wife."

"I don't. I sound completely different," she argued.

"No, you sound just like her, but with a Florida accent. I didn't even know you had a Florida accent."

"I don't have an accent. She does."

"You're right. She's the one with the accent. You sound just like the Zephyr I've always known." He chuckled.

"This is going to be hard."

"It is, but I think you can talk your way out of a wet bag. Nobody even notices you don't answer questions. I watched you do it in the shops today and with Max. I'll have to pay attention to see if you answer my questions," he said.

"I answer your questions."

"Did you see your mom in the house?" he asked.

"When I saw the stairway, I remembered when she told me she had fallen down the stairs and had broken her arm when she was seven. I could see her there with the cast on. She once told me that when her parents died, she couldn't bring herself to go into the house. She could feel them around her, but now they knew all the secrets she had kept from them over the years."

"Do you think she came back after?" he asked. He didn't even know what religion she had been raised in, much less if she believed in an afterlife.

"No, she never came back. She will forever be trapped in Florida," she mumbled.

Exhaustion was overtaking him again, and her smooth, calm words were lulling him into sleep. He wanted to stay up and talk to her, but her words were pushing him into the darkness. With a sigh, he gave in and shut his eyes. Within moments, he was sleeping again.

# CHAPTER TEN

THE CLOCK READ 3:25 when Zephyr's eyes opened. Not wanting to think of what time it was, she lay in the warm bed. Zachary's body was wrapped around hers. The hard muscles of his chest and stomach pressed into her back, and his knees were tucked into hers. Warm breath was moving the hair on the back of her head, sending tingles down her body. Or was it that his hand was under her shirt and cupping her bare breast?

She bit her lip as she willed his hand to move, not away but to caress her. But the hand stayed still. Lying there, she loved the fact that his big hand was actually not big enough to hold her entire breast. It was the first time she was happy with the huge things.

But she had to get up, and he usually got mad when he touched her, and boy was he touching her right now. It was easier to be with him when he wasn't mad at her.

Trying to carefully wiggle free, all she managed to do was have him tighten his hold on her. He pulled her closer to his body with the arm over her stomach. The hand that had been on her breast had moved, and in doing so, his palm had slid over her sensitive nipple, and she almost moaned at the sensation. She had to force herself to suppress her body's reaction to his. It took a few minutes before his body relaxed again, and she was able to break free.

Within an hour, she was showered and dressed in leggings and a comfortable top, snuggled into the chair and opening her computer. Her eyes kept darting to the bed to see if any of her movements were waking Zachary up. So far, he hadn't moved. He was still on his side with his bare chest showing above the covers. The white bandage reflected the streetlight, making it stand out in the dark room.

Zephyr put her headphones on and slid the USB drive into the computer. First, she started the music, then glanced up to see if Zachary could hear, but he didn't move. Then she opened one of the two files on the USB drive.

In seconds, her book opened before her eyes. This was it, the last book. Book number thirteen. It was over. She had written the last sentence weeks ago, and now she had to remove twenty thousand of the words. Ken had said the book was too long. It was the most she had ever deleted from her work, ever. It would take entire scenes to get rid of that many words. What could she cut out, when everything was important? It was like he had asked her to cut off her arm. All of it was important.

When she had started the first book so many years ago, she had known how it would end. The middle took the most work. She could have written this book right after the first. From the beginning, she knew the twists and turns it would take to get to this spot. All of her books were written to point to this ending.

She started reading in the middle of the pages, but the story was so familiar, she knew exactly where she was and where she was going. After spending two hours deleting, typing, changing, and rewording, she noticed that the sun was coming up. She looked at her word count. It was up by over a thousand. Zephyr leaned her head back against the chair and closed her eyes. She was going the wrong way. This was impossible.

Movement caught her eye, and she looked at the bed to see if Zachary was up. Their eyes met over the computer. He was lying propped on his arm, just looking over at her in the chair, all just-woke-from-sleep sexy. His hard chest was still visible and even better looking in the first sunshine of morning.

He smiled at her, and she smiled back. All she wanted to do was throw the computer aside and slide back into bed with him and see what his hand looked like holding her breast like he did the night before.

Of course, the room wasn't actually filled with the sounds of 80s love songs—that was just being pumped into her head. The sights and the sounds were blending in her mind, and she had to bite her lip to keep from moaning.

Watching him climb out of bed, she was disappointed when he slid into his jeans instead of just letting her watch him walk around in his underwear. He walked over to the bed beside where she was sitting. Reaching over, he pulled off the headphones from her head.

"Morning," he said, his eyes staring into hers.

He was so sexy sitting there with no shirt on, just jeans that he forgot to button. His brown skin was shining in the morning sunlight. Her fingers inched to run over his muscles.

"Morning," she managed, but barely.

"The curls came back." He actually touched her hair.

"I know. Patty would be so sad. She said she used enough straightener to flatten the Rockies, but it was no match for this." She pointed at her head.

"It's only wavy now, though. Not ringlets." His hand fell away, but his eyes were still on hers.

"Yeah, good thing I got everything to get it straight again," she replied.

"Are you working? When did you get up?"

"I am reviewing and correcting. I've been up since just before four."

"Two nights in a row, and you've barely slept." There was concern in his voice.

"I don't sleep much. Just a few hours at night is all I need." She shook her head slightly, remembering his arm around her this morning and his hand on her breast.

"Your boyfriends must love that," he said softly.

Swallowing hard, nobody she had dated had made it into her bedroom. "I guess."

"I should get ready for the day. Breakfast will be here soon." He quickly pushed up from the bed and disappeared into the bathroom. He was mad again; she could tell by his walk. Now, what had she done? Was it because he thought she was staring at him? He'd started it.

She saved her work and pulled the USB drive, slipped it into her bra, and shut the computer. Going to his bag, she pulled out the files on her sisters to look at, but a book fell on the floor as she did. Picking it up, she saw it was her book, the first one. She rarely looked at her work once it was completed—she couldn't change it anyway.

Zephyr sat on the bed and opened the book, reading the opening paragraphs. It was like getting a hug from her younger self. Before she knew what she was doing, she had grabbed a pen from the bedside table and was making notes in the margins, changing words.

That's what Zachary caught her doing when he came out of the bathroom. He walked over to her and grabbed the book out of her hands, and looked at the notes. He flipped back a few pages and then looked at her. "You know you can't change it now, right? You cannot change the entire first sentence on the first page."

Letting out a breath in a puff, she said, "No, I can't change it. That's why I don't read them. I see the mistakes and the muddled words."

Turning the book over and looking at the cover, he said, "It says you won three awards for this book alone. I don't think the words are too muddled."

"You don't understand. I see these places, the people, and the words sometimes just don't explain it like I want them to. The first paragraph is kind of green, but it should be green. Ireland, shamrocks, a blade of grass. It's dull, and I don't know how I could make it brighter." She looked at the pen in her hand and twirled it as she spoke.

"But that is the paragraph that's hooked how many people to these books? It's good," he said.

"But not great," she whispered.

"What is really wrong, Zephyr?" he asked, sitting down on the bed. He put the book on the nightstand.

"Nothing."

"Is it this guy stalking you?"

"No, I don't think he's anything," she admitted. Even though he had turned up in her house, she felt he was harmless.

"What then? You can talk to me."

"I have to eliminate twenty thousand words from my last book. That's thirty typed pages. I'm having a hard time getting rid of it. All of it's important." It had been years since she had anyone to talk to about her work. Only Brian had ever cared.

"Holy cow. Can you make it into two books?" he asked.

"No, there's not enough material for that."

"Do you have to end the series at that point?"

"Yes. Everything has all been for this moment," she admitted, peeking up at him.

"So, they finally get what they are looking for. I thought they would get there by the end of book one." He laughed at himself.

"Well, it takes all the books. They get closer every time," she replied.

"Do they get home?"

"No, it ends with them getting the thing." She didn't want to ruin it for him.

He tilted his head at her in question. "Why don't they get to go home?"

"You don't get to go home. Once you leave, you can't go back," she said simply.

"It seems like the story can't be over until they make it back home."

His thoughts made sense, but how would they get home? How long would that take? As ideas consumed her, she twisted the pen in her hands. She stared blankly in front of her, not seeing anything.

She didn't register when he got up or when he kissed her forehead and said, "I'll come get you when breakfast is ready."

# CHAPTER ELEVEN

ZACHARY WAS READING the crazy redhead's book an hour later when Max showed up to make breakfast. Zephyr hadn't come down, and he knew she was in the same spot he had left her. In his life, he had never seen someone turn inward so fast and completely. He asked a question, and her blue eyes started to just stare—they didn't see anything. At first, he was nervous that he had said something, but he soon realized she was plotting a story in her mind.

She was taking the first steps in a journey that a million would follow behind her on. All she had to do was type the words to lead them through her mind.

When Max came in, Zachary had gone up to see Zephyr. She was on her computer, now typing. She hadn't even noticed him opening the door. She had looked up and smiled at him, but her hands did not stop moving. So, he left her to her work.

Back in the kitchen, Max was waiting for him. "Is the Mrs. up yet?"

Zachary smiled at the word, his Mrs., "No, I think I'll let her sleep."

"What do you want for breakfast then?" Max asked.

"I'm a light eater. Just fruit and toast. I can make it later and eat with the Mrs." He really enjoyed saying it out loud.

"I'll leave you to it, then. But I wanted to tell you that there is a farmer's market happening on Main Street this evening. It happens every week, but maybe you two would like to take a walk through," Max said, then pulled a piece of paper from his pocket. "Here's a coupon for the Hart Farms stand if you wanted to get something."

Zachary took it and looked at the coupon, zeroing in on the name. Hart, Zephyr's name. "Yeah, we'll try to make it. Is it supposed to be cold out?"

"You're going to need a jacket. Did you bring jackets?" Max asked.

"No, we forgot them," he admitted.

"Oh, I can bring over a couple later, then. You'll need jackets, but maybe you don't need to buy any. Florida isn't a winter jacket place." Max chuckled as if only he knew it was warmer there.

"Thanks, that would be great."

"Anything else you need?" Max looked around the room.

"Yeah, I'm reading a series of books and am going to finish the first one before I can get another. I hate to leave Zeph alone. She will be working on her thesis all day," Zachary explained, hoping the other man would buy the excuse.

"What series?" Max asked.

"The Traveler series, by Z Connor. Do you know it?"

"No, but I know my nephew has read them. I think the drugstore would have them uptown, about four blocks from here," Max replied.

"Do you think they would deliver?" Zachary wasn't about to leave her alone.

"No, but I can have my brother-in-law bring one over. His office is right next door to the drugstore. I could probably have them here by lunch," Max said.

"Can he grab all of them? Not the first, but the rest? I will pay for the delivery."

"Sure. Jasper isn't busy these days. He's an accountant, and tax season is way off," Max assured him as he left.

Zachary sat back down on the couch and opened the book. Once again, he looked at the first dozen pages with corrections on them and smiled at the neat handwriting. He could see her at fifteen, writing these books in notebooks. Her penmanship showed how many hours she had spent just writing long-hand.

He checked on Zephyr again, who was still typing, but now she had her headphones on and was humming with the music. As he'd laid in bed this morning, he realized she didn't even know she was doing it. It had woken him, and he enjoyed the sound, low and whisper-quiet. It had drawn him out of sleep, and when he had opened his eyes, she was sitting in the chair, bathed in sunlight. It was bouncing off her curls again, and her blue eyes had met his over the laptop. She had been so sexy just sitting there, doing her thing. Her bare feet were tucked under her.

Shaking his head, he went back to reading, letting himself get lost in the world Zephyr had created. He actually felt her on every page, and he felt he was getting to know her better by reading her words. In some way, it felt like he was reading her diary from when she was young.

Sometimes he wondered if she had written these words on the table at the beach house. Was it the weekend he had been there?

# CHAPTER TWELVE

EVER SINCE ZEPHYR had turned eighteen, she had been able to dictate her own schedule. When the story came together in her head, she could write until it was done. She could work all day and night with no issue, then crash when it was finished. Meals turned into quick snacks or ordering out when needed.

Today after Zachary had changed her way of thinking about her story's end, she had started to write. Throughout the day, Zachary would bring up meals and snacks and beverages for her. He hadn't lingered or demanded conversation, just set down the food near her and came for the dishes later.

With her headphones on and concentrating on what she was writing, she hadn't noticed he had come into the room. When she looked up, he was sitting on the bed near the chair she was sitting in. With a start, she gasped.

Pulling her headphones off, she said, "You scared me, Zachary. How long have you been there?"

"A bit. You need to get dressed," he said.

"I am dressed." She gestured at her leggings and T-shirt. It was the same thing she had been wearing when he had woken up this morning.

"Today's the farmer's market," he told her as if it mattered. She had never been to a farmer's market in her life.

"I have to finish this," she argued. It had been years since she stopped before a scene was done. Or, in this case, in the middle of a sentence.

"You will have to stop, Zephyr. You can't miss this because you were doing something you could do tomorrow. Today is for meeting your sisters."

"But ..."

"No buts. You have to pause that mind. Will this pause it?" he asked and touched his finger to the tip of her nose. "Now go get ready. Max loaned us some coats."

He reached to take the computer out of her hand, but she pulled it closer to herself. Without even looking at the screens, she typed some keys and pulled the USB drive out, then released the machine to him. Watching as he took it to the desk and set it down, she enjoyed the view of his firm butt in the tight jeans. Above the jeans, he wore a dark green sweater that clung to him in all the right places.

She quickly grabbed an outfit out of the drawer and hurried into the bathroom. It took more time than she expected to get her hair straight, and she knew she would abandon the practice when life righted itself for her.

By the time she walked down the steps, Zachary was standing by the door with his shoes on, coat in hand. He actually smiled at her, a real smile.

"You clean up nicely, Zeph," he said.

"Zephyr," she reminded him as she tied her brown boots and put on the coat.

As they stepped outside, the cold hit her in full force. Though she had no idea what the temperature was, she knew she had never felt this kind of cold before. Her ears and fingers were immediately frozen.

"Wow, this is cold," Zachary said and took her hand in his as they walked the block to where the farmer's market was held.

As they entered the light-filled open area near downtown, they saw that it was full of tables with vendors selling their items. Zephyr looked around and noticed nobody seemed to be bothered by the cold air, which made her feel different somehow. Like she didn't belong there.

Zachary pointed with the hand that was holding hers. Her eyes swept in that direction and saw the sign for Hart Farms. They were here. She had known they would be but had been a little nervous they wouldn't have shown up. That was her luck.

"We'll just walk past and then go back in a bit. Just look the first time," he whispered in her ear. Somehow, he knew she wasn't ready yet, even though they had been working towards this for days.

A shiver ran through her body as his warm breath blew over her cold ear. He noticed the shiver, and concern shown in his brown eyes.

"Are you cold?"

She looked at him, surprised. "Are you not?"

A laugh was all the answer he gave, but it was enough to relax her a little. She loved his laugh.

Hand in hand, they walked down the row that the Hart Farm stand was in. Zephyr tried to avert her eyes as best she could, but she knew she was gawking. There, talking to a woman buying something was Evie in the flesh. She had blonde hair that was tied back in a braid, and she was wearing a red jacket. She looked like the picture Zachary had given her the day before, but Zephyr tried to see the ten-year-old from the pictures her mom had.

As they walked, Zephyr heard part of the conversation.

"Ben is getting tall," the purchaser was saying.

"I know! I think he'll be taller than Jasper one day. He's already taller than me," Evie said to the lady with the same smile that had been captured by the camera that a young Zephyr spent hours looking at.

"How are the little ones?" the purchaser asked.

"They're good. More active than I remember Ben being." Evie made a gesture with her hands that Zephyr had seen a hundred times in her childhood from her mom.

"You've just forgotten, and now you have two," the woman said with a chuckle.

As the conversation faded, Zephyr had wanted to stop so she could listen more. It was like her mom was talking to her from the grave. Evie had the same tone and cadence as Zephyr remembered. It had been so long since she had heard that voice, she was shocked when it sounded like her mom's. They turned down another row, and Zephyr wondered if Evie had any idea she sounded like her mother.

When they passed the next time, the woman was gone, and Evie was talking to someone behind her. Still holding her hand, Zachary pulled her towards the table Evie was casually leaning against. Zephyr's steps slowed; she wasn't ready yet. She needed more time. Relief washed through her as Zachary pulled her to the table at the stand next to Evie's.

Zachary's breath was hot on her cold ear when he whispered, "Look interested, Zeph."

But she was listening to the conversation going on behind her at the neighboring stand. She could tell by the voices that Evie was talking to one of her sisters.

"Have you decided if you are going to take a vacation this winter?" Evie was asking.

"I don't know if Gabe will be able to get enough time off to do anything fun." *That must have been Zoey*, Zephyr thought. *Her husband's name was Gabriel.*

"At least I don't have that problem. Jasper can get off any time until tax season rolls around. But I would have to pull Ben out of school. I hate to do that, but warm weather ..." Evie said.

The voices rolled over Zephyr as she looked at the items for sale on the table in front of her. A familiar warmth settled over Zephyr at the cadence and tone. A memory rushed through her mind of sitting on the floor in some tiny apartment, playing with toys as her mom talked on the phone. Maybe it was the accent that brought it all back, or maybe it was just the fact that these also were Kate's children. But she hadn't thought about those days in years.

As the feelings were washing through Zephyr, Zachary had been picking up and putting down things from the table. He turned her to him and put something on her head and looked down at her.

Placing a hand over each cheek, he wiped away the tears from her eyes with his thumbs. "Don't cry, Zeph," he whispered.

She shook her head. "I'm not."

"Okay." He softly smiled at her and let her cry.

His words had made the memory fade, bringing her back to the present. He must have put a hat on her head because she was starting to feel warmer. Or maybe it was because his hands were holding her face, and his was a few inches away from hers. She could feel his hot breath on her lips as she stared into his brown eyes.

Blinking, she watched as he closed the small space between them and kissed her lips lightly, just a whisper of a touch that set her entire body on fire. Suddenly, she couldn't feel the cold air at all. She was consumed by the warmth of Zachary.

"Get a room!" someone hollered from somewhere in the distance.

At least it sounded far away. As Zachary straightened up, he looked at the stand behind the one with the hats. Slowly, she too turned her head in that direction to see who had interrupted the moment.

"Yeah, you too. No hanky-panky out here." Zoey was now standing, leaning against the table with potatoes on it. Her brown eyes were sparkling, and she was laughing as she said it. Zephyr had never seen anyone who looked so much like her … ever.

"Zoey, leave them alone," Evie said. "Sorry about her. My sister is a little outspoken."

"I'm sorry, I shouldn't have kissed her, but I really couldn't help it. She looks so beautiful in the hat," Zachary said to the two women.

Both women's eyes then shifted straight to Zephyr, and both said, "Ahhhh."

"Should I buy it for her?" Zachary asked the women, and both nodded enthusiastically. Zephyr watched Zachary smile at the women and turn to pay the woman who was selling the hats, adding one for himself to the bill.

As he was paying for the hats, Zephyr watched the women who were her sisters. They looked very similar, and even though their hair and eyes were different colors, they had many features that were the same. Anybody who saw them would think they were sisters. Would they notice that she, too, looked the same as they did?

"I hope you've tied that one down. He's a keeper," Zoey said to her.

Unable to find words, Zephyr held up her hand, the one that wore her mother's wedding ring—their mother's wedding ring.

"How long?" Evie asked with a smile.

Why hadn't they discussed what they were going to say about their relationship? Maybe they had never thought it would come up, but every time they were with anyone else, it did. Zephyr took a deep breath and let her imagination fill in the gaps her mind could wrap around.

"It seems like just yesterday that I became Mrs. Wainwright. A dream for so long, but a reality for just a short amount of time. Maybe one day, it will feel real," Zephyr said as Zachary turned around.

"Are you from around here?" Zoey asked. "You have an accent, and I have never seen you around before."

"No, we're from Florida, just on vacation," Zachary said.

"Are you on your honeymoon?" Evie asked, looking at Zephyr.

"We prefer not to call it a honeymoon because honeymoons end, and we plan to stay this way forever," Zephyr replied shyly, feeling Zachary's arm encircle her waist and move them forward to the table her sisters were standing at, pushing her closer to them.

"Well, I am Zoey, and this is my sister, Evie," Zoey said.

Zachary introduced them. "I am Zachary, and this beauty is Zephyr."

"That's an unusual name," Zoey said, wrinkling her nose.

"I don't know. I've met quite a few Zachary's in my life," Zephyr said, wanting to deflect from her unusual name.

"I think she means you, Zeph. I have yet to find another Zephyr, but you are one of a kind." Zachary chuckled behind her, still holding her in his arms.

"Thank you, Zachary. My mother liked unusual names. I've had to suffer with it," she said. His arms relaxed around her as she started to relax in the conversation.

Only once had she asked her mother why she had chosen such an unusual name for her. Her mother had said she liked Z names. That was all. It really explained nothing.

"Are you guys staying in town?" Evie asked, satisfied with Zephyr's answer. Maybe due to her mother naming her Evangelina. *Our mother,* she reminded herself.

"Yes, we're staying at a B&B not far from here," Zachary explained.

"Max's place?" Zoey asked.

"Yes, Max Valentine." Zachary nodded. "He gave me a gift certificate for your stand."

"Of course, he did. Since you're staying at the B&B, you must be looking for snacks and such?" Evie asked.

"Yes, and something to go with sandwiches."

"Not leaving much?" Zoey asked suggestively with a wink.

"No, the Mrs. is working on her doctorate, so it's a working holiday," he said, grinning back at her.

"That's too bad. There are a lot of neat things to do around here," Evie replied.

"Don't worry about us; she's on a deadline. I don't know what she would even do if she wasn't writing; it's the only thing she knows." Zachary said, and she could have sworn he kissed her head.

Zephyr stilled as his answer really made no sense. They are going to see right through them. Zachary felt her tense, and his arms went back around her waist, but this time, his hand slid under her jacket and shirt and rested on her bare stomach. His cold hands on her bare skin sent shivers up her spine and heat to her core.

Zoey was eyeing them oddly when a little girl around six came running from out of nowhere and went under the table to hug Zoey. The dark-haired girl was a bundle of energy, and all the adults looked at her.

"Hi, Aunt Zoey. Evie."

"Hi, Molly, where is your mom and dad?" Evie asked the child.

"They're walking really slow. I had to leave them behind," Molly explained.

"And Lily?" Evie asked.

"At a sleepover without me," Molly answered with a touch of anger.

Zoey crouched down. "So, you get your mom and dad to yourself? And you left them?"

"I did. They were walking really slow!" The child complained again.

Evie looked up at Zephyr and Zachary. "Molly is Max and Della's youngest."

Zephyr had watched the conversation with the child but was having a hard time concentrating on anything but Zachary's hand under her shirt. His hands were pressed firmly to her bare stomach. Both were splayed, and his thumbs were touching the bottom of her bra while his pinkies were touching the top of her pants.

Without her consent, her hands found themselves on top of his, above her jacket. She had managed to not lean her entire body into his, mainly just to keep her head upright. Zephyr knew it was impossible to feel his heat through two sweaters and two jackets, but she did.

*It was all an act*, Zephyr reminded herself. An act for the benefit of others to prove they were a couple. Zachary was a very good actor, even though she had a hard time believing that they had barely touched before this moment. All she wanted was for this moment to never end.

Knowing it had to an end, she reluctantly pulled away from his arms. Instantly, her body felt the cold surround her. Was it from the air or the absence of his body?

Seeing Max from the previous night in the crowd, she watched as he walked towards them. He was holding hands with whom Zephyr knew was Della. She looked like the pictures she had seen of the woman on the plane—short, medium-length red curly hair. The couple was holding hands and slowly strolling through the crowd, greeting people as they went.

Sliding her eyes back to the other sisters, who were talking to the little girl still, she saw all three in one place. It actually surprised her how much she wanted to tell them who she was. She wanted to be a part of the family; the family she had been denied by decisions beyond her control. But she still didn't know if they would want her.

She knew she had swayed because Zachary grabbed her by the waist, on the outside of her jacket this time, steading her, reassuring her. How does he always know when her emotions are getting the best of her? Was she that easy to read?

When the couple finally made it to the stand, Della and Max talked to the sisters for a bit before turning to Zachary and Zephyr. Watching her sisters interact, she knew she had missed the opportunity to be a part of the group. Once again, the girls were together, and Zephyr was separate.

"Della, this is the couple staying at the B&B this week. Zachary and Zephyr. I'm glad the coats fit." Max introduced them to Zephyr's oldest sister, who looked so much like her mom. The mom Zephyr knew, but Della hadn't.

"Yes, they are almost perfect." Zachary agreed.

"I was worried that hers wouldn't fit. She's a bit bustier than my Della," Max said, lifting his wife's hand to his lips for a kiss.

"Max, did you really just say that in front of her? Sorry about him. I cannot control what he says." Della turned to her and smiled.

"It's okay. I am a bit bustier than most," Zephyr said with a smile.

"I just meant that she was the same size as my beautiful wife, but bigger. Not complaining, just stating a fact." Max tried to fix the situation, but only dug his hole deeper.

Della turned to her husband and said, "Max Valentine, stop talking."

Zoey was laughing at her brother-in-law. "Max, are you starting to think your wife lacks something?"

Della ignored her sister's question. "How is your stay going? Did Jasper bring by the books you wanted, Zachary?"

"Yes, and thank you for that. I just hate to leave this one alone, even if she's ignoring me to work." He pulled her closer to him.

"Isn't he just so sweet?" Zoey said.

"He knows all the right things to say," Zephyr agreed, wishing it wasn't an act.

"So, Zephyr, Max said you have relatives around here?" Della asked. Her green eyes suddenly on the younger woman.

"No, it was Zachary who said he had relatives around here," she replied, knowing she said had said it wrong, but hated that she lied to them. When she was young, those same green eyes could see through every lie she told. Could Della see through her today?

"That's right. You are working on your doctorate. You don't look old enough to have made it through a master's program." Della was squinting at Zephyr, trying to catch the lie.

"When you are good at something, you can get through a program faster than some people might think. I have some gifts that have paid off for me over the years," Zephyr said in challenge, not answering but telling the truth.

"Sounds like she is smart, Della. You don't have a doctorate, though, do you?" Evie asked slyly from behind the table.

"One day," Della assured her younger sister.

Zoey turned to Zephyr and Zachary and changed the subject completely. "How did you two meet?"

Both were silent for a moment, and Zephyr realized Zachary wasn't going to say anything. It was up to her. "We met on the beach. He was surfing and had just come in and was all wet and sexy. He had just left the Army and was still fit at that time—very sexy. I was staying at a friend's beach house for the weekend, and he was staying at his dad's beach house." No need to mention that it was the same beach house.

"So, he came in from surfing, and I was poking my toes in the water. He asked if I wanted to use his board, I said no. Then he asked if I wanted to go swimming, I said no." She wondered if he remembered that day on the beach. It wasn't the first time they had met. They had actually met three years before, but that was the first day she saw Zachary as a man. A sexy man.

"Why didn't you go swimming?" Evie was hanging on every word.

"I'm scared of the water. I haven't been in the ocean since I was five. I had been caught in a riptide and almost died. I don't ever go in there." She shook at the memory. Zachary's hands tightened on her waist again. "So anyway, we went to his dad's beach house and talked on the deck for hours. That was the beginning. And now, here we are."

What she left out was that they had actually fought like cats and dogs until Zachary stormed off, and they proceeded to ignore each other for the rest of the weekend. With time, Zephyr had realized that no matter what they fought about, it came down to a battle for the love of a man. A man who had enough love for both a son and daughter, but neither could see it at the time. But could they see it now?

"How cute. I love a good love story," Zoey said dreamily.

"How did you and Della meet, Max?" Zachary asked.

Della laughed and answered for her husband. "He ignored me for ten years and then realized I was the love of his life."

"I wasted a lot of time not noticing this one," Max replied and kissed her hand again.

Zoey laughed and said, "Harts accidently find love. It's never as easy as meeting on a beach. There's always a long back story."

"How so?" Zephyr asked. If she and Zachary actually were a couple in love, they had one hell of a backstory.

"Evie here fell in love with Jasper after his grandpa died. But in reality, she had a lot of baggage from her first marriage, but he was so in love with her. Neither was willing to take the first step. A hundred wrong steps were taken before they could take that first right one together," Zoey explained.

"What's Zoey's long back story?" Zephyr needed to know.

"Zoey," Zoey said with a grin. "She found her soulmate, but it took months to realize it. Gabe and I had baggage to unpack before we could see the truth."

"Cryptic," Della said. "In reality, they met during a bar fight. She nearly got arrested by him, and they kept bumping into each other. He dumped her, and then they got back together."

"It was better than that," Zoey said to her oldest sister through pursed lips.

"It was. You guys were pretty cute. But I think he should have arrested you that night." Della laughed at her little sister, who stuck her tongue out at her.

"So, who has been married the longest?" Zachary asked the group.

"Evie had jumped the gun. I was engaged first, but she had to get married first," Zoey complained.

"She was pregnant. Evie's always pregnant when she gets married," Della teased her sister.

"Hey!" Evie argued.

"Don't 'hey' me. It's true," Della stated.

"Are you guys coming out to the pumpkin patch tomorrow night?" Zoey asked.

"I hadn't heard of a pumpkin patch," Zachary said.

"I have one. It's open every evening except Friday night when we are in town. You two should come out. There's a corn maze." Zoey waggled her eyebrows at them.

"I think we'll try to check it out tomorrow," Zachary said. "If I can tear this one away from her computer."

"You got me off it tonight, so maybe tomorrow you will be just as lucky." Zephyr hoped she sounded flirty.

A customer or friend came up and broke up the sister's conversation, and Della and her family wandered off. With the other two busy, she let Zachary lead her away from the vegetable stand.

As they walked away, she realized that she had enjoyed spending a few minutes with her sisters. They seemed nice and fun to be around. Zephyr could tell that they spent a lot of time together and were comfortable with each other and each other's families. She wondered if she could ever be that comfortable with these people, or any people for that matter.

# CHAPTER THIRTEEN

As Zachary walked back to the B&B holding Zephyr's hand, he wondered what she had thought of her sisters. He thought they were friendly and fun. Every once in a while, one would do something that reminded Zachary of Zephyr. Though the girls had not been raised together, they definitely had things in common, from tiny gestures to the cadence of their voices.

During most of the evening, he had tried to be touching her; it was the only way he knew when she was getting nervous. At one point, it had almost backfired when his hands had accidentally slid under her jacket and shirt, and he was touching her skin. At that point, he had not been able to let go of her. Feeling her warm skin had mesmerized him.

Of course, his body had been on high alert since he had kissed her when he saw she was crying. He had just wanted to take away her tears and reassure her but had given in to temptation and couldn't help himself.

Though they had left the Hart sisters behind, he was still holding her hand and couldn't make himself let it go. Her hand was warm in his, and she didn't seem to want to let go of him either.

"So, did you make up the story about how we met on the spot or had you thought of it before?"

"The story was true, except for the sexual tension," she explained.

"Who was the guy in the story?" He looked over at her.

The story had been exciting, and he wished it had been true. In reality, they had met at a fast-food restaurant when his father had said he wanted to adopt the girl. That meeting had not gone well, nor had any of the others after that.

"You. You were home from your first tour of duty. We ended up having a blow-up fight, and we ignored each other the rest of the weekend," she said.

"I don't remember it like that. You were what, fourteen?" he asked.

"Fifteen. I guess we usually ended up fighting, so what was one day compared to another?" She shrugged.

"I was a jerk." He hated that his behavior was so bad when she was around. He was the one who had messed up so much for her.

"Yes, you were. I was too." She squeezed his hand.

"Are you really terrified of the water?" he asked. That part of the story had seemed so real, and now he knew the entire story was true.

"Yep. I don't go in beyond my ankles."

"Really? You own a beach house on the ocean." He had always pictured her swimming every day. It's what he would do if he owned a beach house.

"I should give it to you. You love the place. I just live there," she admitted.

"Dad wanted you to have it."

"He only left it to me because I lived there. He let me move in when I aged out of the system, and I never moved out. I should have bought a place long before he died, but I felt comfortable there. Safe. I should have signed it over to you at the will reading, but you accused me of stealing it, and I got angry. I have a temper," she stated as if he hadn't seen that temper in action.

"I was just jealous, like always," he replied, and the conversation died as they walked into the B&B. They had left the lights on when they left, and now after putting away the carrots and apples they had purchased from the Harts, they went upstairs.

It was still early in the evening, but when they got to their bedroom, Zephyr grabbed the T-shirt she slept in and went to the bathroom. Zachary removed his gun and holster from his leg and put them away. He was happy to be back in the warm house—the air had been chilly during their time outside.

When Zephyr came out of the bathroom, Zachary went in to take a warm shower. Under the hot spray of water, he let his mind wander to the feel of Zephyr in his arms. The sensations spread through his body as he just held her in his mind. When he had touched her bare skin, all the blood had rushed to his groin, and he had just touched her stomach. He had to hold her close in front of him so that nobody noticed.

As he turned off the water, Zachary stopped the thoughts of Zephyr as well. *Hands off. Once this is over, you will not have to see her again for another couple of years. If Ever.* The thought of not seeing her made him a little sad. Would she go back to the lonely life she seemed to live at the beach house? Would he go back to working too many hours on the force?

He had taken off the bandage that had been wrapped around his gunshot wound but was finding it impossible to get another one on it. His arms didn't bend that way. With only his boxers on, he walked out into the bedroom to ask for Zephyr's help.

There she was, curled up in the chair, computer and headphones on. She was lost in the world she'd created. Her feet were tucked under her, and she was only wearing the T-shirt. Walking over to her, he sat down on the bed next to her chair and just watched her. He loved to do that.

The story was consuming her, and she didn't notice him or anything that was going on around her. Her fingers were typing as fast as he had ever seen anyone type. Sometimes she would stop for a moment, then start up again. When she started to hum along with the song playing just for her, he smiled.

Reaching out, he slid the headphones off her head, and their eyes caught as he did it. The blue eyes that met his were big with surprise. The typing stopped, and she closed the laptop.

"Can you help me?" he asked.

"Sure. With what?"

"I need a new bandage put on. I can't do it myself."

Jumping up, she put the computer on the desk and grabbed the supplies he had with him. Sitting down next to him, she turned and said, "Hold out your arms."

"Do you know how it goes?"

Zephyr nodded. "Of course. I saw it yesterday. You want it done the same way?"

"You saw it enough to know how to wrap it?" He doubted that.

"Naturally."

By the time she put the last strip around his body, he was both amazed at her memory and aroused by her touch. The bandage looked the exact same as it did before he took it off.

"How did you do that? How did you remember what it looked like and recreate it?" he asked, looking down at the white strips.

"Photographic memory and puzzle-solving skills. It wasn't hard." She got up and grabbed the laptop again.

"But, you dropped out of high school." He regretted the comment immediately. When his dad had first told him she was dropping out, he couldn't believe his father would let her do that. At the time, she only had a semester left, but she had turned eighteen.

"I didn't really drop out. I just got my GED instead of a diploma. The test was easy, and then I didn't have to waste my time attending school. I didn't realize that you thought I was stupid." She opened the laptop.

"Not stupid, Zephyr, just a high school dropout. But then you didn't need a diploma to do what you love to do," he admitted.

"Zachary." She started to slide the headphones back on. "I know you have a poor opinion of me, and I have learned to live with it."

He would have responded, but she was not going to listen. She was right, after all. Until two days ago, he'd had a poor opinion of her. Though he knew she was successful at doing her job, he thought that she was using his dad and was not very smart. Now he saw she was as smart as the sister who skipped grades and had needed his dad more than he had most of the time.

With a sigh, he got up and put the bandage supplies back in his bag. Walking back to his side of the bed, he slid under the covers. After watching her type for a while, he wondered how long she would be at it. He was starting to see that she really didn't sleep much. When working, she didn't think about eating or sleeping. It was all-consuming for her.

He picked up the second book in her series, stifling a yawn. This afternoon he had finished the first and was already halfway through the second one. It was eerie that she was writing the ending to the story he was currently reading. She was creating a world that he would read years from now. As the typing faded into background noise, he read what had been typed so many years before.

* * *

A LIGHT TOUCH on his chest woke him from a dead sleep. The lights were off, but the room was taking on the rosy glow of sunrise. His heart was racing, and when he saw movement, he grabbed the intruder and slammed them on the bed with a thump. Rolling onto them, he wrestled the object from their hands and held them high above their head, all the while holding down their legs with his lower body.

Below him, the body wiggled and then giggled. His mind cleared as he realized he had captured Zephyr again. Her small body was trapped, and she was wiggling to get free. In the dim light, he looked into her blue eyes. There was no fear in them, just humor that was making her giggle at his actions.

"Again, Zachary," she whispered.

From above her, still holding her down, he watched her mouth say the words, then her tongue slipped out of her mouth to lick her upper lip, then it was gone. With a groan, he lowered his mouth to hers, tasting the spot her tongue had just wetted. Her lips were as soft as they had been last evening in the cold, but now they were warm. The first taste was so good, Zachary had to do it again. This time she answered the kiss with one of her own.

Relaxing his grip on her arms, he pulled one of his back and leaned on it for support while running the other down her bare arm, just feeling her soft skin beneath his fingers. Lowering his head again to her waiting lips, he was rewarded by her mouth, ready for his. As he deepened the kiss, he half expected her to push him away. Especially when he felt her hands pressed to his chest, but then they slid to his back and pulled him closer to her.

Shifting off her legs, he felt her groan and tighten her grip on him. Her grip loosened as he continued to kiss her, and she trailed her hands down his back. Warmth spread through his body at her touch.

Sliding his hand down her body, his mouth left hers to lightly kiss across her jaw and ear. As his lips loved on her soft neck, his hand found their way under the T-shirt she wore, across the stomach he had held not so long ago. Slowly, his hand reached higher and cupped her breast. He had a dream about this the night before, and it was even better in reality.

It surprised him that her breasts were larger than his hand could hold. He had no idea that they were that big. She was so small otherwise.

Returning to her mouth, he kissed her until he felt her moan as his hand brought her nipple to a hard peak. Shifting again, he sat her up and pulled her shirt over her head. With the shirt gone, he could finally see her before him.

When his eyes had swept over her body and back to her face, he looked into her eyes. He could see worry in them. She was worried about if he liked her body. He smiled at her and let out a low whistle, then pushed her back down on her back on the bed.

Lying down beside her again, he ran a finger from her ear to her jaw, turning her face towards him. "You are gorgeous, Zephyr Hart."

At his words, he watched her blush from her breasts to her hairline. Leaning over her, he took a nipple in his mouth and brought it to a peak, then circled it with his tongue. He gently blew on it and said, "I love these."

He then moved to the other one and did the same. This time her fingers found their way into his hair, holding him to her. Leaning back, he slid his hand over the peaks and cupped her breast in his hand again. He just watched his hand, then looked into her eyes. She was watching his hand also. Her mouth was slightly open, and she was breathing heavily.

Suddenly, he kissed her open mouth fast and deep while his hand moved to the other breast. Pulling away, he looked down again at where his hand was caressing her. "I love how pale you are, how my skin is such a contrast to yours. It turns me on. Does it turn you on, Zephyr?"

All he heard in response was a raspy, "Yes, Zachary, yes."

God, he had needed to hear her say it. He smiled, then leaned down and took her mouth again in a deep kiss that had their tongues battling for control. After a moment, he pulled away again and kissed his way down her body. As he made it to her breasts, he slid his hand down her stomach until he brushed over her core, and her hips lifted at the contact.

As his hand slipped past her panties and into her wet folds, he focused his attention on her other breast. Lightly, he caressed her with his fingers as his mouth matched the movements on her breast. Zephyr rewarded him by arching her back as she gasped, calling his name into the early morning light.

# CHAPTER FOURTEEN

HIS FINGERS and mouth were making her body hum, and that hum was turning into a heart-pounding melody as the speed increased. The movement was making her body respond to him, and she was unable to control what was happening. She needed to feel more of him.

He had flipped her onto the bed after she'd tried to take the book out of his hand. She thought she was dreaming when he kissed her, an odd dream since she had yet to sleep. After writing all night, she was going to go to bed, but Zachary was still holding the book in his hand.

Through her unfocused eyes, she watched his mouth on her breast, suckling and circling it with his tongue. As she watched, his eyes met hers in the dim light, captivating her with their darkness. His eyes were consuming her. Zephyr was unable to look away as she felt his finger slip into her core, and she shuttered at the sensations washing through her as she soon came in his arms.

As the shutters continued, he moved his mouth to hers and kissed her, and she kissed him back as best she could. When he pulled away, she collapsed onto the bed, breathing heavily. Slowly, he pulled her panties off her.

All she could think about was him and how he was making her feel. Usually, she could think of more than one thing at a time, but right now, it was only him. She watched him shed his underwear, knowing that there was something she needed to tell him, but she couldn't think of what it was. She was too preoccupied with staring at his erection.

Without her knowledge, she reached for it and slid it through her hand, smooth, soft, and hard. So hard. It was glorious, and she still held it as she slid a thumb over the tip. She was rewarded by a gasp from Zachary, which made her smile.

Sliding her hand slowly down the shaft, she noticed a condom in his other hand. Zephyr let go and leaned back, watching as he slid it on. Biting her lip, she sat up again, but this time she kissed him on the mouth. Their tongues tangled as their hands wandered over each other's bodies.

Their mouths disconnected as Zachary lifted her in his arms and slowly took a nipple into his hot mouth. She grabbed at his head to pull it closer to her sensitive bud and let her head fall back as she moaned his name over and over again.

He shifted them a little, and she felt his fingers slide into her folds again. She was still hyper-sensitive as the pressure started to build in her again. Zephyr gasped, snapping her head upright when she felt his penis start to push at her entrance. With blurry vision, she watched it slowly slide into her, inch by inch. Zachary groaned and pulled back out a little, then went in another inch, back out, then more.

Her breathing was ragged. He felt so good; she didn't want it to stop. Still holding her by the hips, Zachary paused for a moment and hissed through clenched teeth, "Zephyr, are you a virgin?"

"Don't stop," she gasped.

"Are you?" he hissed again.

"Yes. Are you going to stop?" she asked, wiggling her hips to get out of his steel grasp. She didn't know if she was trying to get away from him or make him slide into her completely.

"This might hurt." Was all he said, and he pulled out a little, then pushed in harder than he had before.

Zephyr gasped in pain for a moment, and when it was gone, all she felt was her body surrounding him. He was holding her tight to him until she started to rock her hips, her body wanting more.

Before he started moving, he tipped them sideways and rolled her onto her back, kissing her on the lips. Wrapping her legs around him, she matched his movements and rocked her hips against his.

As he increased the speed, he reached between them and rubbed her sensitive core, making her body shake as she came again in his arms. He soon followed with his own orgasm, his body hard and stiff as he yelled her name.

They both collapsed onto the bed, spent in the morning sunshine. Breathing heavy and unable to move, Zephyr secretly wondered how mad he was going to be at her. Zachary was always mad at her whenever he touched her, and she had forgotten to tell him she was a virgin.

"Zeph," was all he said as he panted on top of her.

"Zachary," she answered, not knowing what to do now.

"Am I hurting you?" He lifted his head to look into her eyes, then smiled at her.

"Just squashing my boobs," she answered with a shy smile of her own.

He rolled over so that he was now on the bottom, and she was on the top. "Can't be squashing those wonderful things."

Kissing her nose, he pushed her hair behind her ears, then gently pulled her head towards him so he could kiss her mouth. It was just a light brushing.

"Did I hurt you?" he asked, still holding her head.

"No. Well, just a little, but then it was gone," she admitted.

"Why didn't you tell me?"

"It slipped my mind. This wasn't on the schedule for today." She folded her arms on his chest, then rested her chin on her hands.

"I guess we did go from zero to sixty a little quickly," he admitted.

"Maybe we were at ten, but the rest went fast. It was nice, though," she said.

Grinning, he replied, "It was *very* nice."

She sighed, and he started rubbing his hands up and down her back. She closed her eyes but then opened them again.

"Did you sleep last night?"

"No, but I got my book done. Number fourteen." Her eyes suddenly felt heavy, and she felt her lids lowering.

"I thought there were only thirteen?"

"Only because there wasn't enough material for fourteen. I took them home now. Because of you." She was talking, but the exhaustion was overtaking her. From the lack of sleep to their recent intense activity, she was going to pass out soon.

She felt him roll them onto their sides and roll her to face away from him. He pulled her into his arms and kissed her ear. "You need sleep."

"No, I'm fine," she said, but she had no idea if he answered

# CHAPTER FIFTEEN

THE BUZZING of Zachary's phone jolted him out of sleep. Opening his eyes, he realized he must have drifted off with Zephyr in his arms. Grabbing it from behind him, he shut off the sound. His eyes quickly landed on her sleeping form, wondering if the sound had woken her. Sliding out from beside her, he grabbed his clothes and left the room.

At the door, he turned back to make sure she was still sleeping. Her eyes were still closed, but when his body had left hers, she had flopped onto her back. Zephyr's red hair was curly again, and it was wild around her head on the pillow. One nipple had escaped the sheet that was covering her, and he longed to go taste it again.

With a silent curse, he shut the door on her and answered his phone. "What is it, Travis?"

"I just got to your place, bud. The firefighters just got the fire out," his partner said.

Zachary had put on his underwear and pants as they spoke. A wave of dread suddenly coursed through his body. Zephyr's books.

"How bad is it?" Zachary choked out.

"The kitchen and garage are gone, most of the living room, too. The back bedrooms have a little damage, but I think it's a total loss."

Zachary made it to the top of the stairs and sat on the landing as he listened. "Can you get inside?"

"No, they won't let anyone in. There's little left, man," Travis explained.

"I need you to get to the spare bedroom. This is the most important thing I'll ever ask you," Zachary said.

"I'll try." Travis had doubt in his voice.

"Call me when you get inside," Zachary demanded.

Hanging up on his friend, Zachary knew his partner would be calling back soon. They had been partners for three years, and he was the closest friend Zachary had. He needed to get Zephyr's books out of the house before they were destroyed … if they weren't already.

As he waited, he slipped on his shirt and wished he was still in bed with Zephyr. Zephyr. His house had burned down, and he couldn't wipe the grin off his face that she had put there. Houses come and go, but Zephyr was forever.

He tried to rein in his thoughts about Zephyr and forever. He wanted her in his life and couldn't see going back to the way things were. Now he had to figure out how to convince her she wanted him as well.

The phone buzzed again, and Zachary answered on the first ring. "Are you in?"

"Yeah, I had to sneak in. I'm here in your bedroom." Travis was whispering.

"Is the safe in the closet okay?" Zachary asked.

"No man, it's open, and your guns are everywhere," Travis said.

"Are there some computer disks and USB drives in there?" He had known the save would be open.

"No, nothing like that," Travis confirmed. They were only files on some cold cases, but he knew what the person was after.

"Can you check the office?"

"Okay." Then a pause. "The computer is gone," Travis said.

"Laptop?"

"I don't see one. Desk drawers are all over the floor."

"I figured. Can you open the closet? Are there boxes on the floor?" Zachary sat down at the top of the stairs again.

"I am not taking boxes!" Travis complained.

"Have they been moved?"

"Doesn't look like it, this guy didn't put anything back." Travis was looking at the mess again in the room, Zachary could tell.

"Can you take out the boxes? In the back corner, left side, there is a hole under the carpet," Zachary asked.

Travis cursed, and Zachary heard the man moving boxes out of the closet. It took longer than Zachary had thought it would.

"I got the gun case."

"Open it up and take out the USB drives. Grab them all. Shove them in your pockets. All of them—you cannot leave any."

"Okay, Zach."

"I got them. What do you want me to do with them?" Travis asked.

"Do you have a safe deposit box?" Zachary couldn't think of a safe enough place for them. Odd, since Zephyr had kept them on a shelf in her kitchen.

"Yes," Travis replied.

"Put them in there until I get back."

"Okay. What are they?"

"I can't tell you right now, but when Zephyr is safe, I'll get you a beer and tell you everything," Zachary promised.

"How is your almost-little sister?" Travis knew the story since he was the one who helped get the information together on Zephyr's sisters. The man knew she was an author but had no idea what she wrote. Zachary could imagine his face when he found out how much those USB drives were worth.

Before answering, the only image that came to Zachary's mind was her sleeping in bed, sexy, exhausted, and spent. "She's great. I can't wait until this is all over. I want you to meet her."

"I knew it! After seeing the sisters, I knew you wouldn't keep your hands to yourself." Travis was still laughing when Zachary hung up on him before he could say anything else.

A few minutes later, Zachary had changed out of yesterday's

clothes and into a clean set. Sitting on the bed, he strapped his gun to his leg. Turning to Zephyr, he brushed a curl from her cheek, then pulled the sheet and a blanket over her. He regretted blocking the view but knew she would get cold without it.

Before leaving the room again, he bent to push a curl off her face and kiss her soft lips. He wanted to crawl back into bed with her, but she needed sleep, and he knew he wouldn't be able to stop touching her if he was back in bed with her.

The decision was made when he heard the door to the house open downstairs. Max was here with breakfast. Leaving her behind, he hurried down to see the host.

To his surprise, it wasn't Max who was busy in the kitchen when he made it there. Della was gathering pots and pans and handing some to the little girl she brought with her. Della heard Zachary walk into the kitchen and looked up. Smiling, and said, "Good morning, Zachary. Zephyr still sleeping?"

"Yeah, she was working on her paper into the night, so I'm letting her sleep," he explained. "Who is this?"

"This is Molly, and she's helping me this morning." Della touched the little girl's head as she walked by her.

"Daddy is sleeping. We didn't wake him," the little girl grinned.

"He needs his rest. So, what are you in the mood for?" Della asked.

"Pancakes?" Molly asked.

"Yes." He turned to the little girl and smiled. "Pancakes sound wonderful."

"I knew it!" Molly replied happily.

As they started finding the ingredients for the pancakes, Della said, "I am sorry about my sisters. They are a little much sometimes."

"That's okay. It was fun to see siblings getting along."

"We do get along, now. Do you have any siblings?"

"Almost once, but no, I'm an only child," he answered, thinking of the woman upstairs.

"There's a story behind that 'almost,' I think," Della said as she let the girl dump ingredients in the bowl.

"Not a good one. I'm adopted, and my father almost adopted a girl once. It didn't happen." Zachary tried Zephyr's method of telling the truth but not saying much.

"That's too bad it didn't work out. My two are adopted. I don't even want to think about what would've happened if it had fallen through." He watched as she kissed the top of the girl's head.

"Did you always want to adopt?" He had to know. She had been twenty-four when Kate had died, old enough to have taken in Zephyr at twelve.

"Yes and no. I wasn't going to have children of my own for medical reasons, but I never really had the urge to go out and adopt. I don't know how to explain it. I wasn't even thinking about the possibility when the girls ended up orphaned, and I was asked to raise them by their grandmother. I knew I had to do it. I knew they were my kids, instantly." She smiled at the thought.

"I understand. It was like an opportunity you never thought about pursuing until it was in front of you, and you grabbed it." Like if they had dropped Zephyr into her life.

"Yeah! It was just there in front of me, and I took it. It was the best decision I ever made." Della started to fry the pancakes.

"You always say your best decision was marrying Max Valentine. He's my daddy." The little girl piped in.

"Life is full of decisions. Some are best; some are worst. And some are worst for you and best for someone else." With the pancakes made, she put a plate in front of Zachary.

"Sometimes, a decision is made that changes everything for good or for bad. But either way, lives have been changed." He stared at the counter, wondering if his father had ever thought to contact the sisters, who were now adults. Seeing this woman in the kitchen with a child she chose to raise made Zachary realize that she probably would have jumped at the opportunity to raise Zephyr. It was in her nature.

How much better would Zephyr's life have been if she had come here at twelve? She would have been raised by a sister who loved her. She would have had a family. She would never know the fear of being alone. Zephyr deserved that.

Della had made enough pancakes for Zephyr for when she woke

up. As Della and Molly walked to the door, she stopped and asked, "My husband would like to know if you would like to play poker today. The guys need a fourth."

"Sure, as long as it can be here. Zephyr will probably want to work."

"He will be happy to hear it. In about an hour, I think."

"Okay, I'll be ready."

"Zachary?" She turned to him. "Whatever happened to the girl your dad was unable to adopt?"

Zachary smiled and said, "I married her."

# CHAPTER SIXTEEN

A CARD GAME was in full swing in the dining room when Zephyr walked down the stairs. There were three men sitting around the table with Zachary, and they looked to be having a great time. If her stomach hadn't been growling, she would have holed up in the bedroom until they left, but she needed something to eat.

Today she had chosen a dark green sweater and brown pants. Though she felt comfortable with her outfit, she was not comfortable with all the men in the house. They were all strangers, she noticed, all except Max from next door.

Then there was Zachary—what was he thinking? She had woken up alone and naked. Was he regretting what happened? Did he want to do it again? She wanted to know, and at the same time, she didn't ever want to know.

Her heart did a flip in her chest when she saw his eyes were on her as she came into view. When she made her way through the dining room to the kitchen, he threw down his hand and jumped to his feet. Putting an arm around her, he steered her through the room and into the kitchen, leaving the men to make comments about Zachary's attention to her.

Once they were through the swinging door to the kitchen, he

pulled her to him and kissed her. Her only response was to melt into him and return the kiss. Being in his arms was as good as she remembered, with his mouth on hers.

"Good morning ... afternoon," he whispered into her ear when he had pulled his mouth from hers.

"Good afternoon, Zachary," she said breathlessly.

Pulling her away from him so he could look into her eyes, he asked, "How are you?"

"Excited. Worried," she said truthfully.

"Book and then me, or me and then the book?"

"Book, then you."

"Congratulations on the book. The series, for that matter." He kissed her forehead. "Don't worry. We need to talk about us. I want there to be an us, Zeph. Do you?"

"Yes, but I was worried you would be mad at what happened."

"I can never be mad at what we did. I hope to do it again soon." He kissed her mouth again, which made her smile.

Was she really in his arms? Was he really kissing her? Was he really saying he wanted to do it again? She almost whimpered when he pulled away from her. "There are pancakes in the fridge. I have to get back."

"Who are those guys?"

"Your brothers-in-law." He smiled at her expression and walked out of the room.

Searching the room, she found the mentioned pancakes, and soon, she was sitting at the counter and eating them dry. Not her favorite, but she had learned to eat and then go back to work. No fuss.

As she ate the last pancake on the plate, she let her mind drift. She had wanted it to drift to a new land for her next series, but it kept going to Zachary. Zachary's hands all over her, his mouth all over her.

It was definitely time to review her book, but first, she had to walk past the men in the dining room. It wasn't that she was scared of them; she was just nervous about saying the wrong thing. Stiffening her spine, she walked out of the kitchen.

Once the guys saw her, one of them said, "Zachary, introduce us to your wife."

Zachary snagged her hand as she walked by. "Zephyr, this is Gabe. He's married to Zoey. This is Jasper, and he is married to Evie. And you already know Max. They needed someone to play a game with."

Shaking hands with them, she saw that they were all friendly. After matching their faces with what she had learned about them over the last few days, she felt her sisters had chosen spouses wisely.

"Good. You guys have fun. I have some work to do." She excused herself as the guys started talking sports. Making her way upstairs, she settled onto the bed and tried to work.

Mostly, she spent the afternoon staring out the window across the room. She let her life play before her eyes, letting herself wonder about what-ifs. What would have happened to her if Charley Hart had said yes to raising her? What if she had known her sisters her entire life? What if her mom had never left here? All the what-ifs led to her never meeting Zachary.

Somehow, everything that had ever happened to her and not happened to her led her to Zachary. Maybe that was the destination she had always been on. Was she truly at the destination, or was this just a stop on the way to it?

Should she tell the women about their mom? They had no idea she had been dead for years. Should she tell them their father knew about her? Should she tell them about her?

Having only met them yesterday, she was already relaxed enough with them to tell them the whole truth. But if she did, would they treat her like a sister? Would she know how to act, having sisters?

She had given up on working and was just listening to music through the headphones when Zachary came into the room. Their eyes met across the room and held as he walked over to the bed and sat down near her feet. She pulled off the headphones and waited for him to talk.

"We've been invited out to the pumpkin patch." He acted like he had managed to get them tickets to a sold-out concert.

"Do we need to go to a pumpkin patch?"

"It's at Zoey and Gabe's farm. The one the girls were raised on. I assumed you would want to go." He was a little concerned with her answer.

"I do want to go; I just didn't know about the pumpkins." She wasn't able to get excited.

"Did you spend the day up here bringing yourself down? You get to spend more time with them," he said, pulling her computer off her lap and taking her hands in his.

"I don't know. The more time I spend with them, the more time they have to figure out that I'm not all that fun," she replied, biting her lip.

"You *are* fun."

"I'm not good with people. I never needed to be. Groups scare me." She was trying not to cry as she admitted it.

"You did pretty well last night." He slid closer to her.

"No, I didn't. I know my weaknesses. My mom never wanted me here. Sometimes, I can feel her disappointment in me, just for being here," Zephyr said.

"You don't know she didn't want you here," Zachary argued.

"I know she didn't. Even if Charley had let her come back, she wouldn't bring me here. When I was nine, we got evicted and lived in our car for five months. She still worked, so I would sit in the car in the parking lot for her shifts. It was hot; that's what I remember. That summer, we had nothing; she sold anything worth anything. We were at the bottom, but in reality, she had a house here that we could have lived in. But she never brought me here because she didn't want me here where her girls were." She looked at the house across the street with tears in her eyes.

"Your sisters lost their mom young and never knew what happened to her. Their dad was cold and uncaring to them. He treated both Della and Zoey like garbage until the day he died. They have scars too; Kate Hart left all her children scarred." He had pulled her into his arms and was rubbing her back.

"She did. They deserve to know she's dead," she whispered through her tears.

"They do, but only when you're ready." He pushed her away slightly and wiped her tears away with his thumbs.

"So, we're going to a pumpkin patch?" she asked.

"Yep. We're riding with Max and Della and the girls," he said, getting up and pulling her to her feet. Before he let go of her hand, he lowered his lips to her still-damp cheeks and kissed each one before gently kissing her on the mouth. With the arm that was not holding her hand, he circled her waist and pulled her tighter to him. "You are beautiful, Zeph, even when you cry."

"You don't have to say that, Zachary," she whispered and looked away from his brown eyes.

With his hands, he turned in her face so that it was looking at him. "No, I don't have to tell you how beautiful you are, but I am going to because you are. Every time I see you, there is something about you that takes my breath away. I loved the long, wild curls that would wrap around my fingers when my hands went into them. I love the straight, sophisticated beauty that you have right now. And I love that it curls up when it gets wet, defying your attempt to tame it."

"It's just frizzy red hair."

"And that's just your hair, beautiful. Tonight, I'll tell you how beautiful the rest of you is." He kissed the top of her head, right on the hair he loved so much, then he pulled her out of the room and down the stairs. They got their coats, hats, and shoes on and waited for Max and Della.

They went outside to wait, and thankfully, it wasn't as cold as it had been the night before. Zephyr was happy that the sun was out. As she leaned against the railing and looked around the neighborhood, Zachary walked up behind her and pulled her back into his body. She leaned her head back against his shoulder as his hands slipped under her coat and sweater to rest on her stomach.

She felt him gently bite her ear and whisper hotly, "Do you know how sexy it is that I am reading a book you wrote while you're writing a book about the same people not six feet away from me? That you're weaving a story as I am reading it. One day, I will read that story, knowing I was watching you as you wrote it."

Moaning at his words and his touch, she whispered back, "Do we have to go?"

The response she got was a laugh, and he quickly spun her around and kissed her. Drawing her tongue out with his, he deepened the kiss until a horn honked nearby. Her eyes were not able to focus as he pulled away and said, "They're here."

The ride to the farm was shorter than Zephyr had thought it was going to be. When they'd left the porch, her body had been keyed up, and it hadn't dissipated during the drive. She and Zachary were sitting thigh to thigh in the tiny backseat of the van. The entire time, he had either held or played with her hand. She got the feeling he loved the fact that their hands were complete opposites, his being large and brown and hers being small and pale. During the trip, he had put their hands together to see how much bigger his was than hers. He spent time analyzing the scars and marks on her hands. At one point, he had slid her mother's ring off her hand and looked at it, then slid it back on.

When they had finally arrived at the farm, there were over a dozen cars in the yard, all families eager to get the best pumpkin. Evie was watching them as they arrived, sitting in a lawn chair by a cash box.

As the group approached her, she got up and gave Della a hug, and then the two little girls got one as well. The girls took off towards the swing set, and the adults were left alone.

"Evie, you remember Zephyr and Zachary, right?"

"From last night, yes." Evie turned to the younger couple.

"Hi, Evie. Jasper was at our card game today," Zachary said.

"Is this where you grew up, Evie?" Zephyr was breathless.

She had always thought she would have no feelings for the place. Her mother had loved it and hated it at the same time. Zephyr had been brought up on stories about both the greatness of this land and the prison it was to Kate. Now she looked around and felt that this was home, the type that you could spend a lifetime somewhere else, but as soon as you took one step on this land, you belonged.

Home. She looked around and wondered if she had said it out loud, but Zachary was talking to the couple and Evie. Zephyr was able to wander off. At this point, she didn't care what anyone thought. She had waited a lifetime to stand here.

Feeling Zachary's eyes on her, she knew she was safe and knew he would protect her. He would let her do what she needed to, even if he didn't understand it.

Fourteen books, thousands of words typed and handwritten, and close to ten years of time, all to describe this place. Every book took place on this farm, a farm she had never seen; never smelled. But it was all here. No matter where the characters traveled, it was here. Her mother had spent years talking about this place, imprinting it on Zephyr's mind.

Slowly, she sat down in the grass and picked a small piece of the short lawn and analyzed it. Smelled it, touched it, tasted it. Then she dropped it in its many friends. She remembered smells her mom would talk about. The air was clean.

Soon, she felt Zachary sit down behind her and pull her to his chest. She closed her eyes and leaned into his strength. "It's okay, Zeph," he whispered.

"Zachary, do you feel it? Do you see it?"

"No, what is it?"

"It's my books. They are circling in the air. This is them. Every word I have written has been about here. It's overwhelming. I hear so many stories written and unwritten. I want to write them all, but they're all coming at the same time. I … I sound crazy."

"You're explaining to a mere mortal how that brain works." He kissed her head.

"All my books have taken place right here, and I have never been here before. I got the stories, and they got the land."

"Maybe that's why Evie never left, and Zoey and Della came back," he said.

"When I woke up this morning, the stories were gone. They had never been gone before. I thought it was because of you, because of what happened."

He smiled at her. "I'm sorry you thought I had taken your stories."

"I was ready to let them go for you, Zachary. I don't need to write another sentence to make it through this life. I make pretty good money." She turned in his arms so that they were facing each other.

"I don't want your money, Zeph," he said.

"Not the point, Zachary. I would rather spend a night in your arms then have the stories circling my head," she said replied, looking into his eyes.

"But now you have new stories?"

"So many more. It's like my mom only took one and stuffed it in me, but there are millions of others floating in the breeze. I just have to grab one and start," she said, reaching into the air and pretending to grab one.

"Are your sisters going to be the main characters again?" he asked.

"You noticed. Do you think anyone else has?" She looked around as if there was a crowd around them.

"I noticed after last night when I met them." He had read enough of her books to see who was who. "They're not the kids their mother left behind, but their personalities are there," he replied, pulling her hat back over her ears.

"Did I make a fool of myself?" she asked. She looked around to see if anyone was watching. Sadly, all three sisters were.

"Yes, but I told them you have never been on a farm before and had always wanted to see one. Maybe they'll buy it."

"Probably not. They probably think I'm crazy." She sighed.

"Zeph, I just want you to know that you look beautiful when your mind has been blown." He leaned forward and kissed her lightly on her lips.

"Quit being so cute, Zachary." But she kissed him again.

He laughed and hugged her to him. "You know you can call me Zach, right? People do."

Zephyr pushed away from him and looked at him closely: his close-cut black hair, brown eyes, straight nose, and full lips that were smiling. She leaned back into him and kissed his lips lightly and said, "I like you as Zachary. I always have. Zachary Wainwright."

"What am I going to do with you, Zephyr Hart? What am I going to do with you?" he whispered into her hair.

Smiling, she said, "Don't call me Zeph anymore."

"How about I say it only when I whisper into your ear?" he added in a whisper, "Zeph."

"Maybe I'll let you get by with it then."

By the time they had made it back to the group, Zephyr's tears were long gone. Zachary had spent time making her laugh and feeling loved. The three couples that had been watching them made no mention of what had happened. They just turned the conversation casual and teased each other.

When the temperature had dropped, the women had all gone inside to get warm. Zephyr found herself sitting on a couch in a cozy living room with her sisters. Some with babies in arms, others without.

The overpowering emotion that had overtaken her outside had not happened inside of the house. When the suggestion that they go inside had come, she had been worried, but the house was only warm and cozy, no emotions.

"Zephyr, Zachary said this morning you were adopted," Della said.

"No, I wasn't."

"I thought he said that his father tried to adopt you?" Della had a confused look on her face.

"Yes, he tried, but I was never adopted. I aged out at eighteen." She took a sip of coffee. She hated coffee.

"Oh, I thought someone else adopted you," Della admitted her confusion.

"Nobody?" Zoey asked over her sister.

"Few kids get adopted after the age of six. I was twelve when my mother died," Zephyr said.

"Didn't she have any family?" Evie asked, holding her youngest, who was sleeping in her arms.

"My mom was an only child, and her parents were both dead. Social services went to her ex-husband, but he was uninterested. It happens." Zephyr shrugged, but her mind was screaming, "Tell them the truth!" Ignoring it, she went on. "You guys were lucky to all have each other."

"We are now. When we were your age, we weren't close at all," Evie said.

"How old are you?" Della asked with a smile of interest.

"Twenty-three." Zephyr told her the truth, no need to lie.

"I was thinking younger," Della admitted, her smile dimmed for some reason.

"Can I ask a personal question?" Zoey leaned towards Zephyr.

"Sure." She was a little nervous.

"How big are they?" Zoey asked.

Both sisters yelled her name in anger.

Zephyr and Zoey just laughed. "F or triple D, and yours?"

"B! Barely, and I want bigger ones. Are they all you?" Zoey wasn't letting it go.

"Yep. They came when I was thirteen and didn't stop until they were this. I've hated them all my life."

"Zachary likes them, though." Zoey winked.

"He is fond of them, but he has said they are not the first thing he notices about me. Which is nice?" Zephyr recalled their conversation in the car in Florida.

"Do you know who your father is?" Evie asked as she burped a baby.

"No, my birth certificate is blank. Mom didn't talk about it," Zephyr said. Her birth certificate was blank, but her mom had once told her the name of her father. Though her to her at eleven hadn't thought much of the same she said.

"I would almost say you're a relative, just missing the curly hair. Maybe somewhere back in your gene pool is a Connor," Della said.

"Not a Hart?" Zephyr asked.

"No, the hair and the shortness came from her mom. She was a Connor," Evie informed her.

Just then, Max stepped into the house and said, "Della, we have to go. The kids are getting crabby." Both Zephyr and Della got up to say goodbye to the others. Della got in a round of hugs, then Zoey turned and hugged Zephyr too. "I think you're my sister too," she whispered. "And I wanted to see if they were real."

Zephyr laughed at the woman in her arms. These women had made her feel so welcome and excepted, things she had never expected from her mom's girls. Zoey's arms held her tight as Zephyr let the warm feelings wash over her. The what-could-have-beens ran through her mind. Slamming the thought shut, she replied, "They are all me, Zoey, and maybe one day, I will let you touch them. You're just jealous."

"You bet I am." Zoey laughed and let her go.

Evie didn't offer Zephyr a hug, but she didn't expect one. Evie had yet to warm to her, and they were still strangers. But then again, Zephyr didn't expect to be friends with any of them.

The drive home was quieter than the ride out. It had been hours since the sun had set, and the SUV was dark. Even the DVD player for the kids was turned off. Instead of Zachary next to her in the back seat, it was Della.

Zephyr could hear the men chatting up front, but the back seat was silent. Uncomfortably silent. She expected the older woman to accuse her of something at any moment.

"So, you guys always hug?" Zephyr tried to break the awkward silence.

"We try to." Della sounded distracted.

"Why?" Zephyr just wanted to hear more about them. Dive deeper into what made her sisters the way they were.

"Evie started it when Zoey came home from the Army. At the time, Zoey was distant, withdrawn, and depressed. She's back to herself now, but that wasn't the Zoey who came home. Evie decided that she needed hugs and that even though she and I weren't depressed, we weren't very happy with our lives. The hugs have made us closer. We'd never been real close growing up," Della explained.

"But didn't you all live in the same house? How come you were not close?" Zephyr felt sad for them because she had always assumed they had each other when she had been alone.

"I guess we were never on the same page at the same time. I graduated and moved out at fifteen. I never came back. When I left, Evie was thirteen. We were only two years apart in age, but we didn't do anything together. By the time Evie was older, I was busy with college. Zoey was always younger, four years younger than Evie even. By the time she got to high school, Evie had Ben and was out of the house."

Della continued, "Both Evie and I were too busy with our lives to see that Zoey was going off the rails. We knew but didn't know … if that makes sense. And sadly, we didn't do anything about it. When she enlisted, we just let her go. The contact we had over the next years was laughable—a call, a letter, but nothing significant. I didn't even meet her plane when she came home the last time. I just told her to come and get my car."

"Wasn't your dad there for you, at least?"

"No, he raised us, but he didn't put forth too much effort. He had no patience for Zoey or me, but Evie could do no wrong. It has made us who we are," she said as the SUV pulled up to the B&B.

Max suddenly slammed on the breaks, and they all jerk forward as the dome light turned on, and Zachary barked out, "Stay in the car."

The door shut behind him, and the light dimmed so Zephyr could see outside the vehicle. Through the window, she watched as Zachary cautiously ran towards the house, then noticed he had his gun out as he slipped into the already open door.

Zephyr jumped when Della said behind her, "Gabe, its Della. Get in here. Someone has broken into the B&B."

Through the phone, she could hear mumbling.

"Zachary went in, and he had a gun. I think he's a cop." Della looked at Zephyr as she said it. She lowered the phone from her ear and asked, "Is he a cop?"

Zephyr quickly nodded and turned back to the house. Was Zachary safe? Is the guy still in there? Who could possibly follow them here?

Sirens blared in the distance and were getting closer as Zachary walked out of the house, sliding his gun into the back of his jeans. Zephyr finally let out a breath. He was safe. She bolted out of her seat past the sleeping children.

Once out in the cold air, she ran to Zachary, and his arms went around her. Pulling her tight against him, he held her until the red and blue flashing lights lit up the night. He was safe.

# CHAPTER SEVENTEEN

WITH HER IN HIS ARMS, the adrenalin dissipated from Zachary's body. When had she started to calm him? Maybe she always had.

His mind drifted back to what their bedroom looked like. Everything they'd brought had been thrown around the room. The furniture had been moved, and the bedding had been ripped off the bed. It had taken him time to try to find the computer he knew was going to be gone.

Zachary knew he was going to break her heart when she learned the computer was gone, which pissed him off. Somebody thought it was okay to steal her work. Who thought so little of her to steal the only thing she had?

Hugging her tighter, he whispered, "It's gone, Zephyr."

"What's gone?"

"Your computer. They stole your computer." He pulled her away from him so he could see her blue eyes.

"That's fine. It's just a computer, Zachary. Are you okay?" she asked. How was she more concerned about him than her work?

Zachary held her at arm's length and looked her in the eye. "What do you mean, 'that's fine'? You have two books on that computer. How many hours of work? Three days ago, you held on to that computer for almost twelve hours straight. And it's okay that it's gone?" He knew he was overreacting. They were her books, after all. If she didn't see the harm in them being gone, then why should he?

"The books aren't on the computer. They never are. They are always on the USB drive," she informed him.

"Where is the USB drive? I will go look for it," he said, wondering if it was still there in all that mess.

"It's not inside. I have it on me. I always do." She smiled.

Without thinking, he brushed his fingers down her body. Not exactly patting her down like a criminal, just a slide over her body. His hands slipped into her pants pockets, back then front.

"You'll have to head north if you're looking for treasure, detective." Her voice was thick as she teased him.

His hands stopped, and he whispered, "How far north?"

"God didn't bless me with this rack to not use it for storage." His eyes dropped to her chest, but his hands didn't look for the device there. "I had no bra for the trip; no storage. I had to keep the computer close."

"I love your breasts more now than I did before. And I *really* loved them before." He pulled her back into his arms.

As they stood holding on to each other, Gabe, Max, and Della walked up to them. The sirens had been turned off, but the lights still flashed, lighting the neighborhood. Zephyr pulled out of his arms to face the three while Zachary grabbed her hand with his and squeezed it.

"What's going on, Wainwright?" Gabe asked.

"Zephyr has a stalker. I didn't think he would find us here." Zachary told the truth. He was really getting tired of lying to these people. They were good people, and he actually considered them friends.

"How bad of a stalker? Panties or more?" Gabe asked, the cop in him knowing the situation could go from harmless to deadly.

"Death threats for a few months," Zachary said matter-of-factly.

"Any idea who?" Max asked as his eyebrows scrunched together.

"No, we haven't been able to find anyone who would want her dead." Zachary squeezed her hand again.

"What else has been done?" Gabe asked.

"He broke into Zephyr's house. They also broke in and started a fire in mine." He felt Zephyr stiffen as his words. He hadn't told her about the break-in or fire. He didn't think she needed the stress of knowing about it. "My partner took your items to his place for safe-keeping," he said to Zephyr, and she relaxed a little.

"And now here? Is he trying to kill her or get something from her?" Max asked.

"Both, I think. I don't want to talk about what he wants, but now it is probably worth more if she's dead." Zachary had tried to piece together who would benefit from Zephyr's death. He hadn't made the pieces fit yet.

"You guys will stay at the mansion tonight. Gabe will make sure there are a dozen cops watching the house. Tomorrow, you can decide where to go from there," Della stated.

"No, we'll leave tonight," Zachary replied. He needed to get her as far from this town as he had from Tampa.

"Sorry, Zachary. Your tires are all flat on your rental," Max said.

Zachary hadn't even noticed that the tires had been slashed. He knew they were not safe as long as they were in town.

"Evie's," Della said.

"No," Zephyr argued.

"Yes. She has an extra room. Nobody will think to look out there, and there is no traffic during the night. Gabe can get cops posted out there. I'm calling her," Della stated and walked away with her phone.

"It will be the best plan for tonight. Evie has a spare room, and Zoey and I do not," Gabe said, looking over to Della, who gave him a thumbs up.

"I don't think Evie likes me," Zephyr said.

"Don't worry. She barely likes me, either." Gabe smiled.

"Me either," added Max with a grin. "At least you're not dating her sister."

They set the plan in motion, and Zephyr helped Della put the girls to bed as Gabe and Zachary went back into the house to gather up their stuff. Soon they were heading back out of town to the Hart Farm, this time in Gabe's car.

The farmhouse had a few faint lights on as they drove up to it and stopped. As they gathered their luggage, Evie stood in the doorway, holding it open for them to walk in. She didn't say anything. Zachary wondered how much information she knew, but figured she knew as much as Della knew.

When they were in the house and Gabe had excused himself to go home, they were alone with Evie and Jasper. Both couples were silent for a moment, looking at each other.

"So, one bedroom or two?" Evie asked. Yup, she'd heard it all, and she had come to the conclusion they were not actually married.

"One," Zachary said. He was not letting her out of his sight again.

"Okay," Evie answered, pushing away from the counter.

"Show Zephyr. I will just walk around outside for a few minutes," he replied and walked out of the house.

As the cold air hit him, he started to take long, steady breaths. This guy was getting the best of him. He could not get his mind around who this guy was or what he expected to do with Zephyr's book. Tomorrow they would head back to Minneapolis and take the first plane anywhere. Maybe he should even take her out of the country.

After he looked around, he went into the house, and Jasper gave him directions to the bedroom upstairs she was in. When he opened the door, he saw she was sitting on the side of the bed. She was still fully dressed; even her coat was still on.

Tears were silently rolling down her cheeks. Rushing over, he pulled her into his arms and said, "Don't cry, Zephyr. It's okay. I'm here. I will protect you."

"I shouldn't have come. I'm putting them all in danger," Zephyr whispered.

"No, it was my idea," he said, opening her coat and pulling it off her.

"I should have said no."

"You did, and I didn't listen," he whispered into her hair. He loved holding her in his arms. It somehow made everything better.

"But I brought him to their door. He would have left if it wasn't for me."

"How do you think he found you?" He pushed her away from him so he could look into her eyes.

"Because they're my heirs."

"Heirs, as in you left them all your money?" he asked incredulously.

"Yes. I had nobody else to leave it to. They'll enjoy it one day. Probably one day soon." He watched her bite down on her quivering lip.

"So, one day out of the blue, they are going to get tons of money? I think they would rather have a new sister than the money, Zephyr." He pulled her onto his lap so that she was straddling his legs.

"I don't know if I know how to be a sister. Maybe they are better off not knowing." Zephyr rested her head on his shoulder, and her arms went around his neck. Wrapping his arms around her, he knew her mother did a number on her youngest daughter.

"When this is all over, we are coming back here, and you will explain to them everything. Until then, you can lie to yourself all you want that they don't want to know you, but you know you need to tell them the truth." Her head stayed on his shoulder. His hand went up the back of her shirt to rest against her soft, warm skin.

Zachary didn't know how long he held her like that, but they stayed that way until he felt the tension leave her. When her body had melted into his, he was able to relax.

She was still straddling him, and his body had noticed her proximity to his shaft. When her body started to wiggle in his arms, he sucked in a breath and said, "Quit doing that, Zeph."

Pulling her upper body from his and leaving her arms around his neck, she replied, "What?"

Her blue eyes looked at him so innocently; he was lost for words when she wiggled again and then winked at him. With a growl, he flipped her over onto the bed so that he was above her. The motion was so fast that her legs had gone around him in the roll. He was worried that he had scared her, and his heart almost leaped from his chest when she started laughing under him.

Staring down at her face, he watched her stop laughing and bite her lip. "What are you thinking, Zephyr Hart?"

"Too much to bore you with," she answered, almost too quietly for him to hear.

"You are never boring. You're the most fascinating woman I know." He touched her chin and swept his fingers up to her hair, tucking a wayward lock of hair off her face.

"Why do you always get mad when you touch me or kiss me?" Her blue eyes bore into his.

"Because when Ken said you were in danger, I knew I had to protect you. That's what I do. But I didn't know how I was going to be so close to you and keep my hands off you." He felt her suck in a breath at his words. "I promised myself I wouldn't touch you like this."

His fingers ran over her mouth as she asked, "Why?"

"Why did I want to do nothing but touch you, or why wasn't I going to?" His mouth followed the path his fingers had trailed. "We hated each other, Zeph. It's the only emotion we shared."

"I don't hate you. We just have a lot of issues," she whispered.

"Zeph, we fought over a man like little kids. He's been dead for two years, and I don't want to fight about it anymore," he said as he kissed across to her ear. "I just want to touch you."

"I don't want to fight anymore either," she agreed as her hands slid under his sweater. She skimmed over his bandage, then lightly ran her nails down his back.

With a groan, he pulled away from her and sat up. With quick motions, he took off his guns, one on his leg and one on the small of his back, and placed them on the nightstand. Turning back to her, he pulled off his sweater and threw it on the floor.

She hadn't moved from where he had left her and had just watched him with her blue eyes. When he turned back to her, she had covered her mouth with her hand, trying to hide a smile.

He pulled the hand off her mouth and kissed the back of it before grabbing the other and making her sit up. He didn't drop her hands as he leaned into her for a kiss. He was only planning a light kiss, but she was ready for him and sucked his lower lip between hers. Zachary deepened the kiss as he held her hands between them.

Groaning, he pulled away from her mouth and dropped her hands, but in one motion, he pulled off her sweater to reveal a pink lacy bra containing her breasts. By the time her sweater made it to the floor, his mouth was on her neck. She shifted her head to give him better access and smoothed her way up his chest.

His hands moved around her, flicked the clasp of her bra, and slid it down her arms. Pulling back, he watched his hands cover her pale breasts. His eyes went to hers, and they were watching his hands on her as well. The light blue was gone, replaced by dark desire. He knew she was as turned on as he was.

Pushing her back onto the bed, he took a nipple into his mouth and heard her purr as he pulled it into a taut peak. Even though her breasts were large, they were very sensitive to his touch, and it turned him on.

Moving to the other breast, he stopped at her mouth for a long, deep kiss. As he pulled away, he mentioned, "I didn't find the USB." Then he took her other nipple in his mouth and suckled.

She was panting as she said, "I hid it already." Zephyr gasped and arched her back for him.

"Next time, I want to find it here." He gently bit her pebbled nipple, and he felt her suck in a breath.

Following down the curves of her body, he slid her pants down her hips, taking her underwear with them. With a smile, he moved back to her neck for a nibble as he felt her undo the button on his jeans and slide the zipper open. She pushed the fabric over his hips, but he took over and removed his jeans as his eyes devoured her body.

He knew he was grinning at her, but he couldn't stop. He had been dreaming of this for years since that day in the hospital room when he saw her in the window light. Why had he been fighting it?

Lowering his mouth to hers, he softly bit her lip, then deepened the kiss until she was panting in his arms. His hand reached her core, and he felt her suck in another breath as he touched her. Would he ever get used to how her body reacted to his touch?

As he slid a finger into her folds, Zachary watched Zephyr's eyes close when he began to gently caress her. Slow, rhythmic motions had her hips straining. Leaving her mouth behind, he took a nipple into his mouth, and her body came around him. She was still breathless, and her body was still humming when he kicked off his underwear and settled between her legs, pushing her hips wide.

Lifting his eyes from her gorgeous body, he looked into her face. Her eyes were wide, and she was slowly shaking her head. Immediately, Zachary pulled back in shock, not understanding why she wanted to stop. It was at that point he remembered he didn't have a condom on. She must have realized it. He quickly grabbed his jeans, snagged a condom out, and slid it on.

By the time he was ready, she had recovered a little. He was surprised when she sat up and pushed at his chest. Letting his body fall, he realized she really didn't want this. As he landed, he covered his face with his hands and tried to figure out what had happened.

His eyes flew open again when he felt her hands on his chest. He focused on her blue eyes that were sparkling in the dim light, watching her climb over his body to straddle him. His hands went to her thighs as she started to grind her hips against his erection. He grabbed her waist and lifted her, then slowly lowered her onto his shaft. Inch by inch, she slid down it until he was completely surrounded by her.

She stayed perfectly still with her eyes wide, looking down at his face. As a slow smile spread across her face, she started to rock. He was holding her hips but was not controlling her movements. As the speed and intensity increased, she moaned and threw back her head. His eyes were focused on her face and the sounds she was making until her hands left his chest and took up her breasts. It steadied their sway, but the scene before him made Zachary's orgasm rocket through him. As his body tensed, he felt her release join his.

Her body collapsed onto his chest. Circling her in his arms, he held her to him and kissed her head as they caught their breath and cooled off. Still huffing, he said into her hair, "I thought you wanted to stop?"

"Never," she replied with a sigh.

"Did I hurt you?" It just crossed his mind that this was only her second time.

"I thought that my boobs were going to fall off at one point, but no." She laughed softly and shifted her head so she could look at him. "Did I hurt you?" She ran her hand over his bandage.

"No, I'm fine." He hadn't thought about his wound all day. He should take the bandage off and just leave it off, but he didn't want to move Zephyr's body.

"Good," she said and shifted to kiss the white bandage.

Goosebumps appeared on her shoulder, so he forced himself to let her go. He excused himself to the bathroom and hoped not to meet anyone on the way since he had only thrown on his boxers.

To his relief, he saw nobody on his way to or from the bathroom. Quietly, he closed the door and saw that she had buried herself under the blankets. Though he was a little disappointed to not be able to see her body again, he was rewarded by seeing her smile at him.

Shedding his boxers, he slid between the covers and turned off the lamps before pulling her into his arms again. He instantly felt her melt into his body, and he kissed her shoulder before resting his head on the pillow.

"I'm sorry your house burned down," she whispered in the dark.

"It's okay; it wasn't your fault. And don't say, 'yes it was,' because it wasn't."

"Are you upset?" she asked.

"Yes, but I have insurance. I'll rebuild." He actually hadn't thought much about his house, not when he was around her.

"But you'll be homeless while you do."

"No, I won't."

"Do you have somewhere else to live? Or you could stay with your girlfriend," she said, but he suddenly felt her tense as if she hadn't meant to say the words out loud.

"Actually, I think you're right. I'll be staying with my girlfriend."

He felt her pull away but held her tight against him so she couldn't leave. "You see, my gorgeous girlfriend lives right on the beach. A little one-bedroom place. We can watch the sun kiss the ocean every night together."

She was still rigid in his arms. Was she listening or just not getting who he was talking about?

"It's you, Zephyr. I am moving in with *you*." She seemed to relax a little but not completely.

"What's going to happen when we get back to Florida?" she whispered.

"I'm going to move in with you, and you are going to edit your book. In a few months, I am going to ask you to marry me, and you are going to say yes. We are going to have a small wedding on the beach, and then we are going to raise some kids right there. We might have to add on to the house, though," he said out loud describing the images that had been floating through his head for three days.

"Zachary, we barely know each other."

"Really? I know more about you than anyone I have ever known. And the rest I will learn over time," he replied, turning her so that she faced him. "I love you, Zephyr Connor Hart."

"What? When?" Her eyes were large in the semi-darkness.

"You heard me, and I think that the love my father had for you was passed to me when he died."

"That sounds ... creepy," she said, scrunching up her nose.

"It's what happened. When I came into his hospital room, I took his hand in mine and knew he was gone, but I still held it for a few minutes. Then I looked up and saw you standing in front of the window with light bouncing off your hair. I instantly fell in love. I got up and walked to you and pulled you into my arms. I knew I wanted you there forever." He smiled into the dark at her.

"That was two years ago. Two years."

"Well, then, we got into this huge fight at the funeral, and I hated you again. You were the Zephyr I hated, and I couldn't find the Zephyr I loved. Until this weekend."

"We are the same person. How are you going to handle that?"

"When we fight, I'm coming back to you now. I'll let you blow off steam, and then I am going to carry you to bed," he whispered and pulled her closer to him.

"Do you think it will work?" she asked, snuggling into his body.

"I think that after a knock-down, drag-out fight, we will have knock-down, drag-out sex." He laughed.

Her only answer was to giggle into his shoulder. He held her as she fell asleep in his arms, red hair spreading across his shoulder as he smiled into the darkness. He thought their future looked pretty bright as he fell asleep.

# CHAPTER EIGHTEEN

WITH THE SPEED of an old sloth, Zephyr slid out from under Zachary's arm. Less than an hour ago, she had tried this move, but she had woken him up, and he had rolled her back under his sexy body to take her again. But now he should be asleep again, sated and exhausted.

But this was the time Zephyr usually got up, so she couldn't lay in bed anymore. Her mind was racing with words and pictures that needed to be written. The next book had entered her head, and she would be unable to concentrate until it was on paper.

*Success*, she thought as she made it to her feet. He really did look gorgeous lying there in the moonlight. And if she crawled back in, he would gather her in his arms and make love to her again. *Win-win.*

Gathering together clothes and other items she would need, she slipped out of the bedroom, praying nobody was up yet to see her walk naked to the bathroom. Zephyr let out a sigh of relief—she'd made it without seeing anyone. A shower was what she needed to clear her head of that man in her room, that man that had completely taken up residence in her head.

Spending the time it took to get her hair straight, she knew this was probably the last day of hiding her curls. Today she'd leave her sisters behind, and she could let the curls take over again. It had only been a few days, and she knew she was going to miss it here.

Zephyr decided once she got home, she would give it a week and then call Zoey or Della and tell them. They did need to know, even if they didn't want to know her anymore. At least they needed to know their mother was long dead.

Leaving the bathroom and slipping back into the bedroom, she grabbed her USB drive from above the picture hanging on the wall, remembering Zachary's face when he realized she carried it in her bra was priceless. He was so cute.

Sneaking downstairs, she spent a few minutes looking for a pen and paper. She eventually found a stack of printer paper in the laundry room, took a dozen pages, and when to sit at the table. By the time the sun came up, she had written on five papers, front and back. Memories of her youth writing long-hand like this came into her mind. Moving to a new blank sheet, she started writing again, but it was stories of her mom before she had died. Stories of the girls they may not even know.

After getting up and grabbing more pages, she continued to write about the good times. Soon she was writing about the bad times too. The drinking and the drugs that had stolen her mother from her by the end. The last page contained the story of her death. She told it like Brian had told her, then she signed it: Zephyr Connor Hart. The name her mom had given her.

Looking around the room, she noticed a tissue box in the corner. Taking it, she removed the tissues and folded the papers until they lay flat on the bottom of the box. Zephyr glanced at her mother's ring on her finger, then took it off and placed it on top of the papers, then added the tissues back into the box. You couldn't tell anything was wrong with it, but one day soon, Evie would find it. Then they would know, even if she chickened out on calling them.

The sun was not yet up when she sat down and started to write the story that had gotten her out of bed. Within a few minutes, she heard footsteps on the stairs and quickly folded the pages she was working on and slid them into her pocket, just like when she was a kid.

If it seemed odd that Zephyr was sitting at the kitchen table in the wee hours of the morning with only a pen and blank paper, Evie didn't say. Evie walked across the room and started to make coffee as she watched the sun come up.

"Do you want coffee?" Evie asked.

"No, I don't drink it. Thank you, though." Zephyr picked up the pen to start doodling on a blank piece of paper.

Evie took a sip of coffee. "Did you sleep well?" Her eyes were boring into Zephyr.

Trying not to blush, but failing, she said, "Yes."

"You're up pretty early. Couldn't sleep with all the excitement?"

"No, it's just that I can get by on less than some people," Zephyr admitted.

"Della and Zoey are that way. I need a solid eight," Evie said and sat down across from Zephyr.

"I didn't know there were others like that," Zephyr said, wondering where she was going with the conversation.

They sat in silence as Evie drank her coffee, and Zephyr doodled … or thought that she was. Looking down, she realized she had been writing. Just words strung together, making sentences. She folded the paper so Evie couldn't see.

"You have very nice handwriting," Evie commented, nodding at the paper she was folding.

"Thank you." She was relieved when Jasper came down the stairs. He took over the conversation with his wife and left Zephyr alone with her thoughts. She should leave them alone, but she liked to listen to their conversations about nothing.

Evie got up to get Jasper coffee and walked past Zephyr's chair. As the older woman walked past, she lightly touched Zephyr's hair. At first, she thought she had imagined it, but knew she hadn't. Having not felt the light touch since she was twelve, she had forgotten her mom even did it. But just the touch had brought back so many images of days long gone. Biting back tears, she wondered if Evie even remembered that her mom did that.

Before the couple noticed Zephyr's tears, Zoey and Gabe and their kids came over, and Zachary woke up. Soon, Della and her family showed up also. There were conversations about where Zachary would take her next, who could possibly be behind the break-in, and many others that Zephyr tuned out.

With the number of people and the noise level in the house, Zephyr needed to get away from it and slipped out the front door into the cold morning. Sitting on the front step, she let the cold wash over her like she usually let the warm ocean breeze in Florida, letting the breeze take away her anxiety.

She had to get out of there. They were doing nothing but deciding her future, and no one even thought of consulting her. It made her feel like she was twelve again, when nobody really wanted her. They were all just trying to find a place for her. Zephyr just needed to get away for a moment to clear her mind.

The door slammed open behind her as Zachary yelled, "What the hell are you doing out here?"

"Just getting away for a bit. Too many people," she explained calmly.

"So, you thought you would just sit out here and let yourself be killed?" He came out and stood in front of her, hands on hips, looking sexy, but mad.

Zephyr tried to control her temper. "Zachary, just leave me alone."

"I can't believe you would just leave. We are trying to figure out what to do next," Zachary said.

"I know you were, but did you think to ask me? Did anyone?" she questioned, looking into his dark eyes.

"What are you talking about?"

"You are planning my life. You never ask me what I want." She stood up. No way was she letting him look down at her, even if he was a foot taller than she was.

"I'm sorry I'm trying to keep you alive." His tone had her temper rising fast.

"Well, don't!"

"So, we're going to do this again?" he yelled back.

"Yes, we are. If you are going to treat me like a child, we are going to do this again."

"How many times do I have to say I'm sorry? I'm sorry I told my dad not to adopt you!" he yelled at the sky into the cold morning.

"That doesn't change anything, and you know it. Do you know how many foster homes I was in, Zachary Wainwright? Fifteen in six years. I lost everything. Kids stole everything from me. They just destroyed it or threw things away. I have one picture of my mom now. I barely know what she looked like." She stepped off the steps and walked up to him to yell in his face.

"That is not my fault, Zephyr Hart. I had nothing to do with it," he hissed loudly.

"If it wasn't for you, I would never have gone through that. *You*." She poked his chest with her finger.

"Me, always me. How can I forget? What about the fact that your dad didn't want you? He signed the papers Zephyr, but no—it's me who's at fault. What about Brian? Maybe he should have tried harder? He never even looked into ..." His mouth didn't say the words, but she knew he was going to say 'sisters' because he waved his hand at the house behind her.

"Brian was doing what was best for me." She defended the dead man.

"Brian didn't want to lose you. If he pushed hard enough, he would have had to send you to your family. I can see that with my own eyes. He knew it too. He made me promise to bring you here the week your dad died. He knew Zeph. They would have wanted you."

"Don't call me that. He did not know." She put her hands over her ears, so she didn't have to hear him.

"Of course, he knew! He knew that those people were nothing like Kate, but he still held on to you. He had you get emancipated as soon as possible because he knew the man was dead. But he couldn't let you go, and he should have."

"No!" She backed away from him, dropping her hands.

"He wanted me to bring you here when he was dead. He brought me to see my mom's grave when I was eighteen. You were twenty-one when he died and still hadn't brought you. Why? Because he was going to *lose you.*" He pointed at her.

"You're lying," she yelled.

"You know I'm not, Zephyr Hart. You know the truth!" he roared over her yelling.

"The truth is that you're still angry that I got the beach house," she hissed as she stomped up to him and poked him in the chest with her fist.

"You mean the house you've been hiding from the world in for five years?" he said more quietly this time as he grabbed her fist in his hand.

"I knew these last few days were a joke." She pulled her hand free and turned and walked away.

"This is the fucking funeral all over again!" he yelled at her retreating form.

Turning, she glared at him. "No, Zachary, this is worse. I thought you loved me this time."

Spinning on her heels, she took off running up the driveway. She heard someone following her, but the person didn't catch her, so she kept running until they did. At the end of the drive, she turned towards the other Hart Farm down the road. Maybe if she got there, she would be overpowered by the place again. She just wanted to forget Zachary and his words.

Her lungs were about to burst when she made it to the exact spot she had been in the night before. Sliding into the grass, she sat with her head down, trying to stop the tears that were overtaking her. She knew he had followed her—it had been days since he'd left her alone. She tried to stop the tears, but Zachary could bring out the temper that she rarely showed.

"You can just leave if you don't want to see me cry, Zachary," she said without looking up. Silence was all that greeted her as she listened for the stories in the air. Only to be met by empty silence.

"Zachary isn't here," she heard Zoey reply.

The other woman came and sat beside her and put her arms around her. "That was intense."

"Sorry, we're experts at fighting. Same fight, different day," she explained.

"But you love him, don't you?" Zoey squeezed her body to her.

"Zachary? For what seems like forever at this point," she admitted.

She pulled away from her. "Are you really a Hart?"

"Yes." She didn't have the energy to lie anymore.

Zoey whispered, "I thought so."

The silence was deafening for Zephyr. Not only were the stories gone, but she had no idea what Zoey was thinking. In all the scenarios of her telling her sisters about her, it was never silence that greeted her revelation. Anger, joy, sadness, but never silence. Deafening silence.

Pushing her sister's arm off her shoulders, Zephyr got shakily to her feet. It was time to go home. Danger was everywhere, and she couldn't outrun it. She had brought danger here, and now was the time to take it away Zephyr had done what she had set out to do: she told one of Kate's girls who she was, and Zoey could tell the rest of them. Now that it was over, she could go on with her life. She now knew that they did not want her, just like their father and mother.

Stuffing the tears back where they belonged, she started back to Evie's house. Zachary had to take her home. He had forced her here, and she would force him to take her home. Then he could do whatever he wanted. She had two books to edit within the next few months.

Looking one last time around the farm where she could have been raised if things had been different, she committed it to memory. Sights, sounds, and smells. But she really didn't need the memory; she already had the spirit in her since birth. In reality, she was glad she had gotten to see it once. It was her home, even if she had never been there. She wished she could have seen it in all seasons.

With a small smile, she knew her next book would be here also. It had started forming in her mind yesterday, and this morning at Evie's table, it had become clear. It was all right here again. But this time, there was going to be a little beach in it, just a little.

Walking away from Zoey, she took the first steps towards her new life, the one where she was truly alone. Now she would not have a hint of Zachary or Kate's girls. It was just Zephyr now, alone.

"Where are you going?" Zoey called from behind her.

"Home." Zephyr didn't turn around.

"But this is your home," Zoey said the words that she had always wanted to hear.

"No, I don't belong here. Kate made sure of that," Zephyr replied. Walking back was going to take a lot longer than getting there, Zephyr decided as she headed towards the road that would take her back to Evie's.

As she passed the barn, she paused. She had never been in a barn. Moving forward, she decided she never would. Oddly, now she was finally getting cold. When she had walked out of the house, she hadn't taken her jacket with her. She was just wearing her white sweater. The fight and her run must have kept her warm enough, but now that the adrenaline was gone, she was feeling the cold seep through her clothes. Zephyr forced herself to enjoy the chill because she was never going to be here again.

Reaching down, she pulled a blade of grass and looked at it. It was green, the green of her books. No, the green she wanted in her books. The color was right there in her hand. Analyzing it as she walked, she tried to find the words to bring this green to her books. It still wasn't there. As she walked onto the road that connected Evie's driveway to Zoey's, she dropped the grass, leaving it on the land it had grown on. She would never capture the green she imagined. The book was published anyway, and as Zachary said, it couldn't be changed.

As she walked, she wasn't paying attention to anything happening around her except the item she was focusing on. She would just have to find that one item that turned the story in the right direction.

Zephyr picked up a rock and slipped it into her pocket. She would keep it and take it back with her. Taking a deep breath, she smelled the air that held no salt or brine. It was so different from Florida. Would she even remember the smell in ten years like her mom had, though she had no daughter to tell about it?

# CHAPTER NINETEEN

After watching Zephyr run from him, he knew he should follow her. He needed to follow her, and not because she was in danger, but because he needed to hold her in his arms. Hold her until the anger and pain were gone and tell her he was sorry. He'd kiss her until she believed him.

Zoey ran past him, following Zephyr down the road. Even he could see the older sister could outrun the younger, but she let her run ahead—not catching her, just following closely. Zoey had a gun and knew how to use it. She could protect her younger sister.

Gabe jogged past Zachary and said, "What the hell, man?"

Zachary followed the older cop as they followed the women. They turned at the end of the driveway, and Gabe asked, "You called her 'Hart.' Is she one of them?"

Zachary knew it wasn't his place to say anything; it was up to Zephyr. He hadn't even realized he had called her that, but he usually called her Zephyr Hart when he was angry. And today, he had been angry. "I can't say, okay?"

"I will take that as a yes. I think your secret's out, though. Once we get her back, she will have to tell," Gabe replied as they turned down his driveway.

What met Zachary's eyes had his heart aching. Zephyr was slowly walking away from her sister. Her sister was yelling at her, but Zephyr was not responding, just walking. Even from this far away, he could see she had turned inward. Just like when her story had changed, she was not really there.

When he stopped on the road, Gabe also stopped, and they watched what was happening. Zephyr was walking painfully slow as she looked around like she was a tourist trying to see everything at once. She stopped at the barn, and he thought that she would turn into it, but she started moving again, occasionally bending and picking things up and looking at them.

All the while, Zoey was behind her, talking to her. But Zephyr was gone; she wasn't hearing her sister's words. As they drew closer to the road, she could hear the words of a concerned sister. 'What's wrong? Just talk to me. Stop.' But the words didn't reach Zephyr.

"What's wrong with her?" Gabe asked.

"Zoey acts out, but Zephyr turns inward. I've only seen it a few times," Zachary said as she climbed the ditch to get to the road where they stood. She didn't see them at all.

"Like yesterday when she just sat there?"

"Yes, kind of like that. But she was happy yesterday."

While he watched her walk down the road, a car pulled up beside the two men who were now just following the redhead. Zoey had stopped trying to talk to her at some point and got into the SUV.

The window rolled down, and Della poked her head out at him. "What's happening, Zachary?"

"She protects herself by turning inward. Zephyr shuts the world out."

"Because of your fight?" Evie asked from the passenger seat.

"No … maybe. I don't know." Zachary just watched Zephyr.

"Great insight. I'm going to take her to my house. Please send protection, Gabe. Zachary should maybe just stay away." Della rolled up her window and drove forward.

Zachary watched in amusement as Zoey got back out of the SUV and shoved her baby sister into the vehicle. For a second, he thought

Zephyr would fight her almost-twin, but she went willingly. Because her will was gone. Because of him.

Had he taken that away, or had the sister said something? Or was it both? Was it a combined rejection that had her protecting herself in the only way she knew how?

# CHAPTER TWENTY

Looking out the car window, she didn't have the energy to look around. One minute she was walking down the road, smelling the scents around her, and the next, she was in a vehicle driving down that same road. She was aware that her sisters were all in the vehicle and that they were talking. No, they were fighting about her.

The fog in her mind had cleared, and she could hear them now. Shutting her eyes, she just listened to her mom's voice fighting with her mom's voice. It was like her mom was yelling at her three times at once. She liked it when they were happy and not yelling at her.

"Please stop," she said, still with her eyes closed. Or maybe she didn't say it, and they just stopped on their own. But she probably said it out loud.

"Are you okay?" Evie asked from the front seat.

"I need to get back to Zachary, so he can take me home."

"No, you don't have to put up with Zachary. We can get you home if you want to go home," Della stated from the driver's seat.

"But Zachary is all I have," Zephyr whispered.

"No, you have us. You're a Hart," Zoey answered, putting her hand on Zephyr's.

"I only carry the name. You three are the Harts. The girls," Zephyr whispered out loud to them. Did they even know?

"I am not a Hart. Charley wasn't my dad," Zoey stated.

"Did he tell you that?" Zephyr asked, finally looking at one of her sisters.

"Charley? No, I found out on my own. Is he your dad?" Zoey took Zephyr's hand in hers.

"Kate always wondered if he would tell you. She always wondered if it would matter one day." Shutting her eyes, she didn't answer her sister's question.

"Kate. Is that your mom's name?" Della asked.

Forcing her eyes open, she saw Evie and Zoey looking at her. Della was driving. Her hand went to the door to open it and roll out of the car. She needed to get away from this situation. They didn't know, and she never wanted to tell them. The door didn't open.

"Yes," she whispered.

"And your dad is Charley Hart. I can't believe he would pick another redhead. But I guess he had a type," Della said from the front seat.

"Did he know about you?" Zoey asked.

"Yes, but he never wanted me. Not as a baby or when Kate died." There. Now they knew.

"Did you know about us? Well, somehow, you did. You came here." Evie answered her own question.

"I know everything about you, Evie. You're the pretty one with the blond hair. You are better at sports than me; you used to follow your dad around like a puppy and asked every question you could think of, even some over and over again. When you were three, you fell off the tailgate of a pickup, and you had to get stitches and had a concussion. That was the year Della went to school for the first time, and you cried every day for a month when she walked out the door." Zephyr let a hundred other memories that were not her own leave her mind.

"I didn't even know all of that," Evie whispered.

"How do you know all that?" Zoey asked. "Charley could not have told you that."

"Kate," Della said, slamming on the brakes. In anger, she yelled, "Catherine! Kate! She was your mother?!"

Zephyr's eyes were wide at her oldest sister's sudden anger. It was the first time she had seen that side of her mom in any of the girls. The fear of her drunk mom came to the surface immediately after so many years. With the car at a stop, she was able to fling open the door and get away, something she had never been able to do when her mom was alive.

Falling out of the door, she knew she was overreacting but couldn't stop herself. But her adult legs couldn't carry her childhood fear away. She fell against the car and leaned against the tire, hugging her legs to her chest.

"What are you doing? The car wasn't stopped!" Della climbed out of the SUV and stood over her like their mother.

"I'll be quiet," she said, tucking her head in her arms. She was twelve again, and her mom's voice was looming over her.

Feeling arms around her, she still didn't look up, nor did she cry. Her body shook, and she tried to send the fear back to the past where it belonged. It had been years since she had felt it, but this weekend had brought up so much. So much she had forgotten.

"She really did a number on you." Della was squatting down in front of her.

"You just sound so much like her," Zephyr whispered.

"I didn't know that." Della ran her hand over Zephyrs hair to calm her. Like their mother used to.

"Did she abuse you a lot?" Zoey asked from beside her.

"Only when she drank. She never hit me. Ever. She just liked to yell. It's been a long time, and your voice is just like hers. It just all came back," Zephyr admitted the dark side of being raised by Kate Hart.

"How did she die?" Evie asked from above them.

"A bar fight. She was just a waitress who was in the wrong place at the wrong time. Shot."

"And Charley didn't want you, so you went into foster care." Della pieced together what Zephyr had told them earlier.

"Yes. Brian tried, but Charley didn't care."

"What about when Charley died? We should have been contacted," Della stated.

"I asked them not to. I was close to eighteen. I had figured out my future by then, and I didn't want to find out that you were like her. Like him. It was better not knowing," Zephyr replied.

"How old are you?" Evie asked.

"Twenty-three."

Evie scrunched her brows in thought. "So, she must have gotten pregnant soon after she left."

"No, she was pregnant when she left. Charley kicked her out because she was pregnant. He didn't believe her that the baby was his. He told her if she ever came back, he would kick you guys out also. She had no way of supporting four kids, so she left you three. You were better off here," Zephyr said as Della pulled her to her feet.

"Life wasn't all that great here," Zoey replied, looking at Della and smiling a secret smile.

"You were never homeless and hungry. You'll never know what it is like to sleep in a car or eat other people's leftovers. To be left home alone at six for hours on end so your mom can work and not pay for a sitter. You were better off here, together."

"But if we were there, you wouldn't have been alone."

"But if you were there, you would not be here today. Your lives are here, and without here, who would you be?" Zephyr got into the SUV because everyone else had.

"Words. So many words," Evie said, but she was smiling.

"Sorry," Zephyr whispered more to the door she had closed then to her sister.

"You and Della can just talk around things all day long," Zoey said, and Della grumbled from the front seat.

"Is your name really Zephyr?" Zoey asked for beside her.

"Yes. She thought it went nice with Zoey."

"It doesn't," Della stated.

"What's your middle name?" Evie asked after shoving Della's shoulder slightly.

"Same as yours."

"Connor, then. At least she gave you that." Zoey turned towards her. "Do you just go by Hart or Connor Hart? Della and I go by Connor Hart. Or I used to."

"Just Hart, I guess. I don't really have a lot of people calling me that." As Zachary said, she hid from the world and was successful at it.

"What do they call you?" Evie turned in her seat to look at her.

Zephyr shrugged. "Nothing. I don't go out much."

"What do you do then?" Della asked, but didn't turn to look at her.

"I am a writer." Della pulled up to the mansion. She saw that there were cop cars everywhere. The sight made her realize she had to leave soon. She had brought this upon her sisters, and they did not deserve it.

"Have I heard of you?" Zoey asked.

"I don't know. I don't know what you read." Zephyr hedged.

"You have to tell me I am your favorite big sister. And yes, I am finally a big sister!" Zoey laughed, putting her arm around her new little sister as they went up the stairs into the house.

"I don't know if you are my favorite." Zephyr joked.

"So, did mom spill the beans on who my daddy was?" Zoey let her go.

"Yes." She bit her lip.

"Who? And who is yours?" Zoey asked eagerly.

"Mine is Charley, and yours is a man whose name I can't remember." Zephyr hedged as she followed the others towards the back of the house to the kitchen. Her mother had once told Zephyr when she was drunk who Zoey's father had been. Though her mom had said a lot of things when drunk, she had only spilled the beans about her affair once.

"You know his name. I know a Hart who's lying to me." Zoey squeezed her shoulder.

Putting her arm around Zoey, she pulled her close and whispered, "Don't you think it's weird that your brother and sister are married?"

Letting Zoey go as the woman stood stock still in the office area of the law firm, Zephyr went into the kitchen with the other two. She'd let her sister process the information. Sitting down at the table, she watched her two older sisters getting coffee cups and starting the machine to make the bitter brew.

A stunned Zoey came in and sat next to her. Zephyr knew that she had never thought the younger sister knew the answer to her question. And she was having a hard time processing it.

"Zephyr, I finally found you!" All heads turned to see Ken Jackson hurry into the room from the office area. Where had he been when they came in?

"Ken, what are you doing here?" Zephyr recovered first. She had last seen her editor last week, and so much had changed since then.

"Zephyr, I have to get you out of here. I thought that Wainwright would keep you safe, but that's obviously not happening," Ken stated as he stopped just inside the doorway.

Getting up from the table, she saw the concerned faces of her sisters. "It's okay. I need to be here for a while longer."

"No, Zephyr, we have to get you out of here. Have you finished the last book?" he asked, looking at each of the sisters.

"Yes, it's done," she admitted, no reason to lie.

"I need the USB drive, and then we have to get out of here." He walked towards her with his hand out.

"I will help you get it out of the safe," Della stated firmly, leaving the spot she had been frozen in and taking Zephyr by the hand.

"Please do. Time is running out," Ken replied and followed them from the room.

In the office, Della went around the desk and opened the drawer to get a key and went to a small safe in the corner. Opening it, she blocked Ken's view of what they were doing, and Della handed her a USB drive. Zephyr slipped a hand up her shirt and pulled out a USB drive and handed it to her sister. Smiling, she hugged her sister. She, too, felt something was off.

"Here you go, Ken." Zephyr handed him the blank USB drive.

"Okay, now we have to go. Where is Zachary?" He barely looked at it as he slid it into his pocket.

"He's probably with my husband somewhere. My husband likes to take long walks around town. It relaxes him." Della lied as they headed back to the kitchen.

"I will call him later then. The most important thing is to get Zephyr out of here." Ken grabbed her arm and pulled her towards the back door.

"Can I say goodbye?" She tried to pull her arm away.

"No, we have no time." Ken pulled her harder.

"What do you want, Ken?" She dug in her heels in the middle of the kitchen.

"To get you to safety," he hissed at her.

"How did you get past the cops?" Zoey asked from behind her.

"I'm her editor. They let me through," Ken stated his title as if he was that important.

"Was it you the entire time, Ken? Did you write the letters?" Zephyr finally managed to pull her arm out of his, almost dislocating it in the process.

"It's time to go, Zephyr," Ken hissed again, not answering her question.

"No, I don't think I am in any danger here." She sat down on a chair.

"There is a man who is trying to kill you!" Ken tried to grab her arm again, and she jerked it away.

"Why?"

"Because of who you are," Ken explained.

Zephyr shook her head. "Nobody knows who I am."

"A lot of people know," he insisted.

"No, nobody really knows. I know, Zachary knows, and you know. Not even your assistant actually knows who I am." Zephyr's mind started the puzzle she had been putting off for days.

"More people than that know." She knew he was lying to her now.

"But nobody cares who I am. Who benefits if I die?" Zephyr questioned him from her chair.

"Zachary Wainwright," Ken stated with a smirk.

"No, Zachary gets the beach house, and that's nothing."

"These women," he said very quietly.

"But they don't know. Evie, who am I?" She looked at her blond sister, the one whose husband had bought her books for Zachary.

"You're Zephyr Hart?" Evie answered in question.

"Della, if someone dies, does the executor of the estate have to contact the beneficiaries?" she asked the judge.

"Yes, that is the law," Della confirmed.

"Right away?" Zephyr stood up and took another step away from Ken, who was standing too close to her.

"They're supposed to." Della nodded.

"What if they don't?" She pushed her sister for the answer.

"Please, Zephyr. Zachary is your executer of your estate. Is he not going to contact the heirs?" Ken didn't let Della answer.

"Zachary would, which is why I chose him. But if he's dead, then that job falls to you." She pointed at him.

He sneered. "Really, Zephyr?"

"Did you try to have him killed? He was shot a few weeks ago. Was that you?" Everything started falling into place.

"I don't know what you are talking about." He lied again; she could just tell.

"You stand to gain control of my estate if I die, especially if Zachary dies before he can contact the beneficiaries," she explained, solving the puzzle.

"*Absurd.*"

"Were you going to kill my heirs? Their families? For money?" She looked around the kitchen. They were all there except Zachary, who was near.

"I don't need to kill you for money, Zephyr. I make a lot of money from you already," Ken stated with a smirk.

"But I make more. And I can be gone tomorrow if I want to be." She folded her arms as the answer was so obvious.

"You wouldn't leave my company!" His face turned red in anger at the mere thought she would leave.

"Looks like I'm going to. You want to kill me."

"You can't leave me. I have all of your work. All of it!" He tapped his pocket.

"What you have is three books that I have copies of, so you really have nothing. And I have no idea what you have in your pocket, but it is not the last book." Zephyr looked at his pocket.

"Where is the last book?" He looked around the kitchen.

"Zachary has it." She lied.

"Well, now I *will* have to find him. Because I am tired of giving you money for all my work," Ken hissed.

"Your work? *Your* work? I've been writing those books for eight years! Most of my life. You are just the person who gets them into people's hands. I am the one who created them." Zephyr got to her feet to yell at him. She would not be looked down on by this man.

"You were just a scrawny kid with nothing when you showed up at my office," Ken pointed out. It was true, but she wasn't that kid anymore.

"It was not nothing. It has made more money than anything you have ever published." She took a step towards him.

"That's what makes it mine. I published it, and once I get you taken care of, I can become you, and we can finally get that movie made." Ken almost laughed.

"Really, a movie? And you can't become me," she stated firmly.

"You said it yourself. Nobody knows who you are. Nobody even *cares*." He pointed to her.

"Why didn't you kill me in Florida?" She had to know. Wouldn't it have been easier?

"I needed Wainwright. I needed to get rid of him also. I tried, but you got away. Once you two were gone, I could finally get everything changed over to me. It didn't matter about the will once the only person who knew who you are was gone. I would have it all." Ken smiled and pulled a gun from under his jacket. "But now I have the opportunity to kill your heirs. I will do that also."

"But they have heirs. The money will roll to them." Zephyr looked at her sisters, who were scattered across the room. There was no way to protect them all from this man and his gun. Zoey was right behind her to the left, so Zephyr took a step in that direction to block her from the gun. Della and Evie were further back, almost not in the kitchen anymore.

"Grant Miller," Della stated loudly into the room. Neither sister looked at her for saying something odd, but Ken did.

Taking a deep breath, Zephyr rushed at him, throwing herself onto the gun in his hand. It must have taken him by surprise since his eyes jerked back to her, and she heard him curse. They were close when she started toward him, and she was almost touching him when she heard the gun's loud report in the room. It was louder than she had ever imagined. The light that flashed from the end of the gun surprised her. But what took her breath away was the intense pain. It was everywhere all at once. Then it was gone, and so was light and sound.

# CHAPTER TWENTY-ONE

Zachary stood waiting outside the mansion with Gabe and a few other cops. On the way to town, Della's SUV had stopped, and all the sisters had piled out. In his heart, he knew they were getting to know their new sister, but he wanted to be there for Zephyr as well. Over the past few days, he knew that there were things she had not told him and was probably telling them.

Gabe had most of the cops in town and an ambulance on the case. Yes, he knew someone was after her, but were they that close? The town was so peaceful; he couldn't see anything bad happening here.

"So, you have no clue as to who it could be?" Gabe asked for the hundredth time.

"No idea. Should we go in?" Zachary stared at the house.

"No need, the mansion has a voice alarm system. All the sisters know what words to say to get the cops in an instant." Gabe smiled. "Della used to get angry husbands showing up to beat her up all the time."

There was a crackle on the police radio from the car behind them. Instantly, Gabe was heading for the door, along with half the cops that were there. Zachary followed and was right behind Gabe when he pushed open the front door. It looked exactly the same as it had been when he and Zephyr had shown up just a few days ago. The only difference was the sound of a gun going off, something he'd heard many times before.

They followed the sound to the kitchen area. What met Zachary's eyes had his blood run cold. Zephyr was on the ground with red covering her white sweater, and her eyes were closed. The man standing in the middle of the kitchen was Ken Jackson. He had his hands in the air, and Zoey had her gun trained on him. Gabe also had his gun on him.

Once Zoey saw Gabe enter the kitchen, she dropped hers to the table and slumped to the ground to her sister. Zachary holstered his gun and ran to the women on the floor.

Zephyr's white sweater was covered in blood. Had he even told her she looked nice in the sweater? Of course not, he was too busy being a cop instead of being the husband he wanted to be.

Helplessly, he watched as Zoey checked for vital signs and then ripped off her flannel shirt, popping most of the buttons off in the process. Rolling up the shirt, she pressed it to the oozing wound.

Zachary took her hand in his, kissed it, and said, "Zephyr, stay here and listen to the stories. I know you can hear them. Are they floating around us? Do you hear them? Are they whispering, or are they yelling? Can you hear the first sentence? Can you hear the end? Just stay with us and listen to them."

He knew he must have sounded crazy to everyone in the room, and he didn't care; he wasn't letting her go that easily. He had to fight for her. If that meant using her weakness for words, he was going to use it.

Kissing her hand again, he saw her eyes open a tiny bit and close again. Then he heard her say, "I'm listening."

Tears began running down his face. The other cops must have been taking care of Ken because Gabe squatted down to assist his wife. He, too, had pulled off clothes to compress the wound, but every piece that was used was completely soaked by the time another was ready.

The ambulance crew was taking over, and they tried to push him away, but he wouldn't let go of her pale hand. It was paler than usual. Smaller.

"The ambulance will take you to the hospital in town but will then airlift her to Minneapolis," Gabe stated, pulling him away from her.

As the EMTs got Zephyr onto a stretcher, Della handed him a USB drive. "Zephyr gave it to me, but I think you should take it. We will be there as soon as we can."

Zephyr was unconscious as she was rolled into the ambulance, and Zachary climbed in after her. She remained that way through the ten-minute drive and the thirty-minute flight that took place next. The blood also continued to flow. By the time they landed, she had more tubes running through her than Zachary could imagine. He never wanted to see her like that again.

Now he was waiting in the waiting room alone. So far, a nurse had come and said Zephyr was in surgery to remove the bullet. Gabe had called him saying that they were coming, but also that Ken Jackson had confessed to it all. He had been trying to kill Zephyr because he was going to assume her identity. To his surprise, he had also confessed to hiring someone to try to kill Zachary a few weeks before—the man who had shot him.

Zephyr had just woken up when he was able to see her for the first time. Tubes were still stuck in her arms, and she looked so pale, but her eyes were alert. His heart was pounding as he approached the bed, and he let out the breath he was holding when she smiled at him.

Taking her hand casually in his, trying not to touch the tubes, he leaned down and kissed her gently on the mouth. If he hadn't been so close, he would have missed her hoarsely say, "I guess makeup sex is out."

"Just on hold, Zephyr. Just on hold," Zachary said.

"I love you, Zachary. I'm sorry," she whispered.

"I'm sorry about what I said. For everything I have ever said," he replied but noticed she had fallen asleep.

Would they ever get over their pasts? They had left Florida with nothing but the baggage from their histories, and it had almost destroyed them. Would that get in the way of a future?

Sitting by her bed, he held her hand until the nurse informed him that they had visitors. Reluctantly, he let go of her hand to see her sisters. He would keep his promise not to tell them anything, even though he was sure she had told them herself.

After her family walked in, the nurse informing them of her health, that the bullet had been removed, and that it had done little damage, just a lot of blood loss. She would only be in the hospital for a day or two. Della had insisted that when released, Zephyr was to come to her house. There was no way she should travel any further. Evie argued that her house would be better, and Zachary left them arguing about who would take care of Zephyr after her release. Zachary knew they would have had the same fight over who was going to raise her when she was twelve or seventeen.

Zoey left her sisters and followed him down the hallway. Stopping him, she asked, "We want to see her."

"No, she's sleeping now." He hated to say it, but he wanted Zephyr to know when she had visitors.

"When she wakes up then," Zoey stated, and he said he would come and get them when Zephyr wanted to see them.

The doctor was in the room when he entered, and Zephyr was awake. He was on his cell phone, and she was watching him talk. Ending the call, the doctor said, "Okay, it is arranged. We will airlift you to the airport, and a private plane will take you to Tampa. Two nurses will travel with you."

"What?" Zachary demanded.

"Ms. Hart says she wants to go home, and she is willing to pay for it," the doctor answered as two nurses came in, starting the whirlwind that took them back home.

# CHAPTER TWENTY-TWO

ONCE THE DOCTOR came back into the room, she requested to be transferred to Tampa ASAP. Since her credit card was in her room, she just handed it to him, and he took care of the rest. The only thing she wanted was to be home, back in her house. After another helicopter ride and a private plane trip, she was back in hot Florida. An ambulance had picked her up and brought her to a hospital nearby. She had to spend a day or two more before she could get home.

Zachary had been there the entire time. He was not happy with what she had done, but he had let her do the decision-making. Maybe he was changing. Maybe there was a chance of a future with him after all.

After sleeping on and off most of the previous day, Zephyr woke up before the sun came up that morning. Turning, she saw Zachary sitting in a chair next to her bed, holding her hand. A smile tugged at her lips as she watched him. He was still in jeans and a sweater that had her blood on it. Even after almost twenty-four hours in the outfit, he looked good, but maybe a little warm in a sweater.

He must have felt her watching him because his eyes slowly opened. Seeing her smile, he smiled back at her. He leaned towards her and said, "Good morning."

"Morning," she answered.

"Feeling better?"

"No, but less tired," she said truthfully. "What happened, you know, after?"

"After you were shot? Zoey pulled her gun on him until Gabe came in and arrested him," Zachary explained.

"I didn't know she had a gun. Why did she have a gun?" she asked in confusion. Zoey didn't seem the type who would know how to handle a gun. Or even want to.

"Zephyr, she was in the Army, remember? You saw a picture of her in her uniform."

"Oh, yeah. Sorry, I forgot. I'm sorry, it was all my fault. I messed up."

"No, I brought up the past. I know what happens when I do."

"I don't blame you for what happened all those years ago. I don't blame Brian either. It had to happen that way. I needed to be raised by people who didn't care if I showed up to supper or not. If I slept or not. I wouldn't be where I am now if someone had thought that I shouldn't just be writing all the time," she explained what had come to her while she was with her sisters.

"If I had been raised by Brian or even one of the Harts, they would have had me in therapy to talk about why I turned inward when the times got tough. Why I just wanted to tell my stories. Instead, I was able to turn inward and just write them as they came. It was hard, but it brought me a lot. I would probably just be finishing college now and looking for a job. A job I would never love, a job that was just a job. Instead, I was able to finish what I started over eight years ago. And that story will let me spend the rest of my life how I want. Once I get a new editor." She smiled a little.

"How do you want to spend it?" he questioned carefully, taking her hand.

Zephyr bit her lip and looked into his brown eyes. "There's this guy who wants to move in with me, and I think I am going to let him."

"Are you? Seems sudden." His smile was gorgeous.

"I know, but I have been in love with him since I saw him on the beach when I was fifteen. He was pretty hot then, and he's only gotten better," she admitted.

He ran a hand over her hair. "Sounds pretty serious."

"When he asks me to marry him, I have to say yes. He told me so." She smiled from her pillow.

"What about when you fight? When happens then?" he asked as his hand slid across her cheek.

"He promised knock-down, drag-out sex, and I am looking forward to it." She was actually laughing.

He crushed his mouth to hers, and she didn't hesitate to respond to his demands. Hearing him groan, she felt shivers run through her body. As she reached up to touch him, the pain that shot threw her chest, making her swear into his mouth. "Fuck!"

"I assume that wasn't a request." He pulled away from her, chuckling.

"Why didn't you say this hurts so much?" She frowned at him.

"I didn't think you would get yourself shot." He kissed her forehead and sat back down. "What are you going to do about the girls?"

"I'll have to contact them when I feel better. Maybe go up there again."

"You ran pretty fast from them." He sat back down.

"I have a feeling that they'll understand. It seems like we're all that way," she said and closed her eyes.

"I'll go with you. They do love you." He knew that even though they hadn't known her long, all three of the sisters were going to except Zephyr for who she was.

"I know."

"Of course, you won't be getting rid of me that easily." He kissed her forehead.

"Good," she whispered as she drifted off to sleep with a smile on her face.

# CHAPTER TWENTY-THREE

A LIGHT BREEZE blew a red curl across Zephyr's cheek as she watched the waves crashing on the shore from her chair on the deck. She had finally been released from the hospital yesterday. No more nurses and doctors coming and going, just home and peace. Well, except Zachary, who was still hovering.

This afternoon she had finally convinced him to run some errands. First, he was going to see his boss about turning in his resignation. He had decided she needed a bodyguard. Zephyr knew she wasn't in any danger anymore, but if it meant Zachary was around more, she was for it.

Then he was going to stop and visit his partner, tell him about what happened, and get Zephyr's USB drives back. Tomorrow she had to find a new editor. It wasn't going to be very hard since two had somehow already contacted her since Ken's arrest, and it looked like she was going to be able to get a better contract than she already had. Both had even mentioned the movie deal that had been rumored about for a few months.

She was hoping to have a few hours alone with her thoughts, but before she could really relax, she needed to call one of her sisters. She had run as fast as she could away from them, and they needed an explanation. They needed the truth.

She picked up the cell phone Zachary had gotten her while she was still in the hospital. He said he'd call her on it, and he already had when he had gotten in his car to leave for his errands. Earlier she had programmed in the numbers that she had for her sisters. Flipping through the numbers, she tried to decide which to call.

Zephyr took a deep breath for courage but instantly felt a sharp pain shoot from her side at the movement. It was getting better, but not as quickly as she had wanted it.

Leaning her head back to rest on the back of the chair, she stared at the blue sky. Was it snowing in Minnesota? She had wanted to see the snow. Maybe she would have Zachary take her up there later in the year. Maybe she should just show up on their doorstep and not call. Perhaps it would be easier that way.

Knowing she was being a coward, she tossed the phone on the table and looked out at the waves again, but her view was blocked by three people in shorts and T-shirts. Actually, it was her three sisters blocking her view.

Sitting up straight, she winced at the sharp pain that shot from her side. Holding her side and breathing shallow breaths, she watched as Della walked up and threw a picture on the table in front of her.

Her oldest sister demanded, "Is this you?"

Picking the picture up, Zephyr looked at the half-grown girl with red, curly hair and blue eyes. She had never seen this picture before. She had seen so few pictures of herself from her childhood. "Yes, I think so."

"Think?" Evie asked, raising an eyebrow.

"I have never seen this picture before, but I don't have a lot from back then." As she said the words, the three women sat in the chairs around the table.

"How did Charley get it?" Della asked.

"Brian must have sent it, hoping that seeing a picture of me would make him change his mind. It didn't work."

"Fat chance of that." Zoey huffed.

"Sorry I ran," Zephyr said.

"I think we all understand. Hart's have a hard time with happiness," Zoey replied with a laugh.

"I wish we had been contacted when you were twelve. I would have raised you. Evie would have raised you," Della said.

Sitting up straight, Zephyr took her hand in hers. "I don't. I know now that if I had gone to Minnesota or even if Brian had adopted me, I wouldn't be here today. I mean, I would be somewhere, but not here. I needed to be me without restrictions that good parents would have put on me."

"Did you act out and get in trouble like me?" Zoey was curious.

"No, Zoey. You went outward, and I went inward. You acted out, and I shut the world out."

"I don't know which would be worse," Della said

"Neither is worse; neither is better. I am who I am because I could just do what I wanted to do."

"Write?" Zoey asked and pulled out some folded pieces of paper from her pocket and threw them on the table. They were the story she had started at Evie's house. "I read it. It's very good."

"I thought the hospital had thrown it out. Yes, I write, since forever. I love it, and I don't want to do anything else, and I don't have to. But Della, you would have had me hospitalized if, at sixteen, I had stayed in my room all summer just writing in notebooks. But in foster care, nobody cared, and I wrote my second book that summer. Start to finish, editing included," Zephyr stated, looking at her sister.

She continued, "Evie would have forced me to graduate from high school even if I had just received an advance on my first three books. Instead, I took the GED test and got out of school when I was eighteen. I didn't need a diploma. I was never going to college."

"So, you are not working on your doctorate?" Della asked.

"No, Zachary lied about that. I was just working on my last book."

"Last?" Zoey asked

"Sorry, last in the series. I've started another one already." She smoothed the papers on the table in front of her. She was already twelve pages beyond these words.

"But wouldn't a loving family have been better than that?" Evie asked.

"Yes and no. I realized that you three received all of Kate's great features. Some I had forgotten over the years. Evie and Della sound just like her. I can shut my eyes and see her talking when I hear you. That's why your yelling got to me so quickly for no reason. Zoey has her energy, which was mostly gone when she died. The day I was shot, Evie, you walked by me and touched my hair. I had forgotten that she did that. I had forgotten so much of the good but remembered so much of the bad. You guys reminded me of that." Zephyr looked up at the sky, trying not to cry.

"And why 'no'?" Evie asked.

"Because then I wouldn't have Zachary today. And I want Zachary."

"All for a man," Evie said wistfully, and the other two groaned at her.

"Was your book really on that USB drive?" Della asked.

"Yes, but it was actually two books. Thank you for taking that. If I was dead, he would've looked for it on me, but not you."

"Okay, dead. Was it worth it to kill you?" Della asked.

"Yes," Zephyr said. After seeing the contract offers, she had realized how much she was worth; how much Ken had actually stolen from her over the years.

"And we're your heirs?" Della asked.

"Yep. You get everything except the house." She pointed to it behind her.

"Why?" Della pushed.

"Because you're Kate's girls. I may not have been raised with you, but you were raised with me. We celebrated all your birthdays and holiday's as if you were there. Every event I had was compared to an event you guys had already had. She talked about you all the time. I know you better than I know myself. Did you find the letter I left? I thought that you guys would want to know more about her and how she thought of you and wanted to come back." Zephyr wanted to know, and Evie nodded.

"But she didn't, did she?" Zoey stated.

"No, she didn't."

"Is the estate worth anything without the house?" Zoey looked around the tiny house on the beach.

"Have you ever heard of the Traveler series by Z Connor?" Zephyr asked the table.

"Of course. Ben loves those books. We brought the copies Zachary's forgot with us," Evie stated.

"That's me. I wrote that series." Zephyr nodded, then wanted to laugh at the shocked faces that were staring at her. Having actually told so few people of who she is, it always seemed weird to see their reactions.

"They're making a movie about that series!" Zoey's eyes were wide.

"That might be in the works." She hadn't agreed to it yet, but maybe.

"You have the dreaded curls." Zoey smiled from across the table as if she just noticed them.

Zephyr touched her hair. It hadn't taken long to return to its natural state, especially in the Florida humidity. "Yes, all my life."

"Now that we know about you, we are not letting you go." Della took Zephyr's hand in hers.

"I don't know if you'll want me. I am not really like you. I am not very outgoing or fun. I write because I can do it alone. I like to be alone because I am not good with people," Zephyr said.

"I think that we all know you enough to know we'll get along. You are more fun than you think," Zoey said with a wink.

"That's what I keep telling her." Zachary appeared from the side of the house and leaned onto the deck rail. "Hello, ladies."

All three greeted Zachary and chatted briefly with him. Zephyr watched how comfortable he was with the situation. He was looking like his old self with a pair of board shorts and a soft T-shirt. As she had recovered from her gunshot wound, he had removed his bandage altogether.

Turning to her, he said, "Zephyr, can we watch the sunset together tonight? Or do you want to stay here and watch it from here? It's our anniversary."

Biting her lip, she stood up and asked, "What anniversary?"

Walking over to her, he took her hand in his, kissed her lightly, and said, "One week ago today, we watched the sunset from this very deck, or you did. I was over there. I want you with me this time." He kissed her again.

With her hand in his, she let him pull her onto the warm sand. For a moment, she thought she was being rude to her guests, but then that faded. They could wait. Though he was still pulling her, she stopped when her ankles were in the water, then took one more step in. He was testing her boundaries, and she was letting him push a little at a time. Then she stopped and dropped his hand.

Turning to her, he pulled her in his arms so that he had her pressed to his chest. His warm hands were resting under her shirt on her bare stomach. "Has it already been a week?"

"I'm hoping this coming week is even better than the last," he said. "No stalkers, no shooting, and no big trips."

"Just stay here and spend time together? Sounds like a letdown." She leaned her head against his shoulder.

"I think in about four days, I am going to pick a fight with you so we can yell a little, then have makeup sex." His voice and words sent shivers up her spine. Hopefully, her wound will be healed a little more before this fight.

Both stood in silence as the sun kissed the ocean and slid slowly into the water. Reds, oranges, and yellows were aglow in the sky beyond them.

"Thank you, Zachary, for coming back into my life to protect me."

"Thank you for letting me … barely."

"I love you."

"I love you, too."

They stayed there until the sun was gone. When they turned back to the house, the sisters were still there. Last week, they were alone in the world. Today it seemed there was a whole family that wanted them.

# EPILOGUE

In Minnesota, they say it can get too cold to snow. Apparently, that wasn't negative ten, because that was the temperature outside the plane, where it was actively snowing. Not the fun, big flakes in the movies but little ones that pounded against everything. Zephyr couldn't take her eyes off the stuff. This wasn't the first time she had seen snow since she met her sisters, but it never got old. It did get cold, but not old.

They had been back a few times over the last fourteen months, and the families had come out to visit them. They had all come to attend the wedding that Zachary and Zephyr had on New Year's Day last year and had come again in April to escape the snow that Zephyr loved so much. Zachary and Zephyr had gone up for Thanksgiving and then again in February to see the snow, and again in June for Zoey's birthday. After that, Zephyr had to spend more time in California than she had ever planned.

It had taken close to a month to pick a new editor after Ken's arrest. The two offers had turned into eight, and then they started to counter each other. The best offer she received was the editor she chose, with the agreement that nobody would know who she was and that she wouldn't ever have to tour. Since then, they had spent more time promoting her books than Ken had ever done, making her already popular series even more so. Part of the agreement she had was to let them make a movie that had taken a long time. With writing a script and making sure everything was going according to what her mind had seen, it was exhausting. Or maybe that was because, for most of this last year, she had been pregnant and exhausted.

Zion Hart Wainwright had been born just before Christmas, and he was worth it. He had been named after his grandfather Brian, with a twist only Zephyr could add. Now at three weeks old, he was making his first trip to Minnesota, his first visit with his aunts. At first, she hadn't really wanted to start a family right away, but things happened, and ready or not, he was coming. He mostly looked like his dad, but so far, he had the bright blue eyes of his mom. Della said that she thought he had reddish hair, but Zephyr saw the baby every day and felt her sister was imagining it.

"Did you tell them you were coming?" Zachary asked from beside her. He was white-knuckle driving towards Zoey's house in their rental car. He was completely out of his element, driving through the blowing snow that was sticking to the roads. He was gorgeous and hers.

"They always have lunch together on Sunday. Evie said today was at Zoey's. It is nice that they get together all the time." The close they got, the faster the snow came down.

True to their words, Zephyr had become a sister that day on the beach. They called or texted almost every day, and though they had very little shared memories, Zephyr had all the memories from when they were very young. And slowly, they were gaining more memories together, one of the first being that Zephyr had to get a tattoo of a heart even though she was still recovering from a gunshot wound. But the others had one, so baby sister did too. She had let Zachary decide where to put it, and he suggested on her right wrist—her writing hand because she had always written about them.

"You didn't even tell them. What if the car goes into the ditch, and they don't know we are coming?" He kept himself from yelling at her; the baby was sleeping in the back.

"You won't go in the ditch," Zephyr stated and looked over at her husband. Her husband, Zachary. Sometimes she wondered if Brian had somehow known that they would fall in love one day, that he was the link between them even when they didn't get along. But every day, she knew he was watching them and was happy that they were together.

"Snow, Zephyr!" he said as if it were a bad thing.

"I see it too, Zachary." She reached over to touch his tense shoulder and massaged it through his navy sweater.

It had actually taken longer than either one of them had thought to get past the fighting since it had been so natural for both of them to just fall back into the same old fight. But over time, the past had dropped away, and the fights were easier to dissipate before they got too bad, usually by one or the other suggesting that they finish the battle in the bedroom, and that always worked.

"How far now?" he asked. She had the GPS on her phone.

"Two miles," she said as she turned it to him. The destination was listed as 'home.'

Though her home with Zachary would always be in Florida, where she came from was now a farm in Minnesota. Though she had not been raised there, it felt like home.

In Florida, her home had changed when she got pregnant. Zachary had insisted that the beach house was too small for more than two. It was also too small for two. So, he had taken it upon himself to find them something bigger, and Zephyr had not been happy. She loved the beach house. To her surprise, he had talked the next-door neighbors into selling their large four-bedroom house to them, and they kept the beach house. Now she just worked there, and it was her office. And it was perfect.

"I think I see it." Zachary sighed with relief.

"Can I walk from Evie's drive?" she asked, grabbing behind her for her coat.

"No."

"Yes."

"You will freeze to death."

"You'll save me." She liked to remind him of his job: keeping her safe.

"I can't save you from yourself," he mumbled.

"Zachary," she stated firmly. "I want to be in it for a minute. So far, I haven't asked much of you on this trip."

He grumbled and stopped close to the end of Zoey's driveway, not Evie's. He understood what she was saying, and she loved him for it. It had taken him time to get used to her disappearing into her mind. Even though she always came back, she just let her surroundings take her away.

Over the year, how she wrote had changed. No longer was she able to just write until the writing was done. Now he made sure she stopped for breaks and for meals. Also, for walks on the beach and to spend time with him. She had only been able to write one book in the new series. It had been a lot slower going than before, and with Zion, the next was going to be even slower. But he was worth it; they both were.

Swinging open the door, she climbed out, and he drove away into Zoey's driveway and up to the house. After slipping on her jacket and hat, she shoved her hands into her pockets since she had no mittens.

It was cold and windy, and the snow hit her face, causing a tiny bit of pain before it melted on her skin. The feeling was crazy and weird, but Zephyr loved it. Walking towards the house, she looked at all the white. The snow made the other colors pop, the red of the barn, the brown of the trees, the gray of the house, and the blue of her rental car. The color was amazing, and she now knew why white was associated with cold. Snow was cold.

As she walked, she reached down to pick some up, but when she touched it, she realized she couldn't pick it up with her bare hand. Her weak Florida hands were made for touching sand.

Her toes were colder than she had ever felt them, and her fingers were too. She wondered if she had frostbite; her sisters would know.

She knew they were watching her. They always were. Like she was something amazing and unusual all at the same time. Over the last year, she had decided to not be someone different with them or Zachary. She was Zephyr Hart Wainwright, and she would be who she was, no hiding.

Every time she came to the farm, Evie's farm, or the mansion, she went for a walk to think, smell, and feel. It made her more connected to the place where she should have been raised. Every time she came away with more depth for the stories she wrote. Last summer, when they had come, she had finally found the words for the green she had wanted in her first book. It was here the entire time.

The sisters were coming towards her. They were bundled up against the cold even more than she was. Looking up at the dark gray, snowy sky, she wondered if Kate was watching. Was she seeing her girls all together? Did it make her happy? Her sisters' arms encircled her, and she felt like she was one of them, like she belonged. She was finally one of Kate's girls.

**Thank you so much for reading Keeping her Safe. Did you love it? Reviews mean everything to indie writers – you can review Falling for Keeping her Safe on Amazon and Goodreads here!**

Did you fall in love with the Hart sisters? Are you going to have a hard time letting them go? Are you wondering what happened to Della's baby? Will Ben and Clementine fall in love? Are there other series that don't include a Hart that i have written?

Click here to sign up for my Newsletter.

As a bonus, you will also get sneak peaks of all my new books, and you will get a glimpse into my real life and sometimes there were will be mini horses.

Visit my web page for more information WWW.ALIEGARNETT.COM

# ABOUT ALIE GARNETT

I love to read and prefer a little spice in those books. I am lucky enough to live on a small hobby farm in northern Minnesota with her husband and two kids. I enjoy spending time in the pasture with my two mini horses and one fainting goat (who doesn't actually faint). When I'm not writing, I'm busy trying to do all the things I didn't get to while writing. Or maybe I wouldn't have gotten to them anyway, because its laundry, dishes and fun things like that.

# ALSO BY ALIE GARNETT

<u>Indulge</u>

Craving Winter

Enticing Aurora

<u>Landstad, ND</u>

Invisible

Irresistible

Impulsive

Insuppressible

Intriguing

Imperfect

Irreplaceable

<u>The Great Lovely Falls</u>

Falling for the Single Mom

Falling for his Best Friends Sister

Falling for the Boss

Falling for his Step-Sister

Falling for his Fake Wife

Falling into a Second Chance

<u>Hart Series</u>

Seeing her Pain

Her Favor

Max Valentine is Looking at Me!

Keeping her Safe

<u>Stand Alone</u>

Romancing the Doctor